MW00977797

Anon

by Kate Robin

A SAMUEL FRENCH ACTING EDITION

SAMUEL
FRENCH
FOUNDED 1830
NEW YORK HOLLYWOOD LONDON TORONTO

SAMUELFRENCH.COM

ISBN 978-0-573-66307-9   Printed in U.S.A.   #3713

IMPORTANT BILLING AND CREDIT REQUIREMENTS

ANON. was first produced by The Atlantic Theater Company, New York, NY, Neil Pepe, Artistic Director, Mary McCann, School Executive Director, Andrew D. Hamingson, Managing Director. The production was directed by Melissa Kievman with the following production staff and cast:

Set Design: Chris Muller
Lighting Design: Tyler Micoleau
Costume Design: Anne Kennedy
Sound Design: Eric Shim
Casting: Telsey + Company
Production Stage Manager: Adam Ganderson
Production Manager: Eric Southern
General Manager: Melinda Berk
Associate Artistic Director: Christian Parker
Press Representative: Boneau/Bryan Brown

Cast (in alphabetical order):

RACHELLE	Caroline Aaron
TRIP	Remy Auberjonois
JANICE	Susan Blackwell
BERT	Bill Buel
BECKY	Shannon Burkett
RITA	Saidah Arrika Ekulona
CLAUDIA	Dana Eskelson
ALLISON	Michelle Federer
CORRINE	Katy Grenfell
MARY	Linda Marie Larson
PAMELA	Jenny Maguire
GINA	Kate Nowlin
TRISH	Danielle Skraastad
GRETCHEN	Anna Foss Wilson

CHARACTERS

TRIP. Mid 30's. Urban. Charming. Smart. Seems straightforward.

ALLISON. Mid 30's. Intensely positive. Smart. Seems together.

RACHELLE. Mid 50's. Determined. Devout. Catholic.

BERT. Mid 50's. Virile. Struggling. Devoted.

QUALIFIERS

GINA. Early 40's. Earthy. Effortlessly sexy.

BECKY. Late 20's. Upbeat. Totally made-over.

GRETCHEN. Early 30's. Suburban veneer, but been through it all.

PAMELA. Mid 20's. A good girl. Very pregnant.

CLAUDIA. Late 30's. Together business woman.

CORINNE. Mid 50's. Simmeringly angry, but laughs it off.

TRISH. Early 30's. Urban spitfire.

MARY. Late 40's. Gentle, ordinary.

JANICE. Mid 30's. Monied bohemian.

RITA. Early 50's. Sophisticated. Academic. African-American.

The Qualifiers can be played by as many as 10, or as few as 3 actors playing several roles. In either case, it is crucial that there be an ethnic and age range represented by the actors cast.

PLACE

Manhattan and Queens

TIME

Now

Scene One

*(**TRIP** 's loft. Rich. Sprawling. Under-furnished.)*

ALLISON. Where is she?

TRIP. Uh…I don't know. Under the bed, maybe….

(He leads her to the bedroom. She squats by the bed, looking underneath it.)

ALLISON. Ps. Ps. Ps. Here, kitty, kitty, kitty. *(pause)* Can you help me out here?

TRIP. Cat! Come on honey. Come to Papa.

ALLISON. Cat? That's creative.

TRIP. It's direct.

ALLISON. Well, she's not coming out. Let's take a look at the box.

(He looks at her blankly.)

The litter box?

TRIP. Oh. Yeah.

(He leads her to a closet. She looks in.)

ALLISON. Oh my god.

TRIP. It's usually much better.

ALLISON. Well. No wonder.

TRIP. No, really. It rarely gets like this.

ALLISON. Well, it's like that today.

TRIP. I was out of town on business and I just got home in time for you –

ALLISON. Cat likes a tidy box, Trip. Requires it, really. If you let it get like this, she's going to keep going on the bed. How often do you go out of town?

*(**ALLISON** takes a plastic bag out of her purse and starts scooping pellets of cat poop into it.)*

TRIP. Rarely. And if it's more than a night, I have someone stop in.

ALLISON. Well, "stopping in" isn't exactly loving attention.

TRIP. It's not that often. I thought cats were supposed to be sort of independent.

ALLISON. There's a limit. It's a very very damaging mythology, this idea that cats have no needs. They're living creatures! No one is designed to live alone.

TRIP. Don't moose live alone?

ALLISON. No! I don't think so. Do they?

TRIP. I thought. I don't know why. I remember that. They live with their mothers for a year, and then they live alone.

ALLISON. Hm. Moose. Well, cats aren't moose. Mooses? Moose. Cats. Domestic animals, have been socialized, they're not in the wild now, you've made her dependent on you.

TRIP. Not me, personally. Society has.

ALLISON. Well, you've played your part. You made a vow, when you took this animal into your home, it's like being a parent. You give up your right to self-destruct when you become a parent.

TRIP. Really? I wish someone had told my parents that.

ALLISON. I know, me too. But, officially, one should. It's the same with a pet, you give up your right to be self-involved. You've got someone who depends on you. She can't clean her own box. So she pees on the bed.

TRIP. But she never used to.

ALLISON. You said you moved recently? That's very stressful. Cat hates change. Where did her box used to be?

TRIP. In the old place? There was a yard. We kept it out there.

ALLISON. A yard. Oh, poor Cat. She lost her yard.

TRIP. I had to move.

ALLISON. I understand, but they're so responsive to their environments. Even emotionally. People don't realize. Did anything else change? Emotionally?

TRIP. Well, there was a girlfriend. With the yard.

ALLISON. Oh. Well. Were they close?

TRIP. They were. She really. She loved the cat.

ALLISON. Cat is grieving, Trip. Cat lost her mother.

TRIP. She wasn't her mother! She was just a friend. The cat is mine. I love her too. Just as much. More!

ALLISON. Okay. I'm just saying, you can see why she's upset.

TRIP. Yeah. *(He sighs.)* She is upset. *(He seems a little upset now too.)* She used to be such a happy cat. She would never hide this long. She was social! She played! All the time.

ALLISON. I don't see a lot of toys.

TRIP. They're all…they end up under the furniture.

ALLISON. You need more. Would you consider getting another cat?

TRIP. I guess…won't that just make it worse though?

ALLISON. It could at first. But if you get a much younger male, she's less likely to feel threatened. And it could really make things more fun for her when you're not here.

TRIP. I just…I've heard so many stories of two cats who live their whole lives avoiding each other in the same house.

(ALLISON hands TRIP the bag of poop.)

ALLISON. Okay. If that feels like too much for you right now, there are other things we can do.

(She sits at the table and takes out a pad.)

ALLISON. More attention. Obviously. I suggest you start talking to her. And not like she's an idiot. But like she's your friend. Confide in her. It'll be good for both of you. More toys. There should be toys all over this house. You can't spoil a cat. Tidy box. Appealing box. That means a LOT more litter in there. Vigilant scooping. Whenever she goes in there, you come right in with that scooper. Get rid of this plastic one. It's crude. You need a metal scooper. Give it two weeks. Call me with questions.

TRIP. That's it? More toys and a tidy box?

ALLISON. Loving attention. *Metal* scooper. I wrote it all out for you. *(She hands him the paper.)* Call me next week and let me know how it's going. *(pause)* It's two hundred for the house call.

TRIP. But you haven't even met the cat.

ALLISON. I don't need to meet her. I met you. I saw the box. I know a lot about this cat. She's lonely. And she hates the name Cat, by the way. It makes her feel very generic to you. Objectified, even. Like she's just playing some kind of role.

TRIP. Do you want to have dinner with me sometime?

ALLISON. Okay.

TRIP. How about now?

ALLISON. Now?

TRIP. Yeah. I'm starved.

ALLISON. Uh…. Okay.

TRIP. Yeah?

ALLISON. Sure. Fine.

(TRIP hands her the money.)

TRIP. Hey, let's, it's a beautiful night. Let's order in and eat on the terrace. I've got an amazing view.

(He walks her to the terrace. They step out. The view is amazing.)

ALLISON. Wow.

TRIP. Right?

ALLISON. Yeah.

TRIP. Chinese? Thai?

ALLISON. Chinese is fine.

TRIP. Do you know what you like?

ALLISON. Excuse me?

(He picks up the phone.)

TRIP. Do you need to look at a menu? Or can we order now? I'm starved.

ALLISON. Oh. I like snow peas. With tofu.

TRIP. Okay. *(on phone)* Hi. It's Trip at 169 Reade. One order of snow peas, a lemon chicken, some fried dumplings – *(to* ALLISON*)* you'll eat some of those, right?

ALLISON. No.

TRIP. Okay. Shrimp toast? *(Looking at* ALLISON *again. She shakes her head.)* And pork fried rice. *(to* ALLISON*)* We can share that.

ALLISON. I'm a vegetarian.

TRIP. *(on phone)* Oh, wait! Vegetable fried rice? *(She nods.)* Yes. Thanks.

(He hangs up.)

ALLISON. Did you say tofu? With the snow peas?

TRIP. Yeah. Sorry about the shrimp toast. But is that really meat? It's barely even food.

ALLISON. The shrimps were alive once.

TRIP. So were the snow peas.

ALLISON. The shrimps had consciousness.

TRIP. And the tofu didn't? As a young soy bean? You don't think it felt pain?

ALLISON. We all have to draw our own lines. Did you order the tofu?

TRIP. Yes, yes, I ordered it. Do you want something to drink?

ALLISON. I just didn't hear you order it.

(He looks through the cabinets.)

TRIP. I did. I think I have some red wine someone gave me…

(He finds it and holds it up.)

Is this okay? I don't really drink.

ALLISON. You don't?

TRIP. Not much. Why, is that good?

ALLISON. No, it's just, my last – so many people drink too much.

TRIP. I guess. Really?

ALLISON. I find. You don't? Just a lot of people who, you know, have to get drunk every night.

TRIP. I don't know. That's not really my thing. I'll have a glass every now and then. So, do you want some of this, or…what?

ALLISON. Hang on.

(She reaches for the phone.)

TRIP. What are you doing?

(She hits redial.)

ALLISON. I'm pretty sure you didn't say tofu. I'll have a glass. I didn't mean the occasional glass of wine –

*(**TRIP** opens the bottle.)*

TRIP. It's good for the heart.

ALLISON. In moderation, yes.

(On the phone, slightly over-articulating.)

Hi, we just called. Trip from 169 Reade? Did we order tofu with those snow peas?

*(**TRIP** pours the wine in two glasses.)*

TRIP. Yes.

ALLISON. *(on phone)* No? Okay, well, could you add that? With the snow peas. Snow peas with tofu, yes. Thank you so much.

(She hangs up with a triumphant smile.)

TRIP. She must not have heard me.

ALLISON. You didn't say it.

TRIP. I know I said it.

ALLISON. So, you're incapable of admitting you're wrong. Is that what I'm dealing with?

TRIP. Oh Jesus. I thought tofu. I felt tofu.

ALLISON. But you did not say tofu.

TRIP. Okay. Okay. It's possible. In all the excitement, I might not have said what I was thinking, with so much…commitment.

ALLISON. Well it couldn't have been that much commitment.

TRIP. Okay, I don't want you making a mental note on this. I know how women are.

ALLISON. How are women?

TRIP. With the lists. The Pros and Cons.

(ALLISON smiles.)

TRIP. How am I doing? Pro/Conwise?

ALLISON. You're doing fine.

TRIP. No really. Tell me.

ALLISON. Litter box, Con. That you called me and didn't just give Cat away, Pro. Tofu, Con. Terrace, Pro. Shirt, Pro. Pants, Con.

TRIP. What's wrong with my pants?

ALLISON. They're pleated.

TRIP. They're Armani.

ALLISON. Nonetheless.

TRIP. Go on.

ALLISON. Job, Pro. Late, Con. Energy, Pro. Attitude, Con.

TRIP. Whoa. What's the difference between energy and attitude?

ALLISON. The energy is playfully seductive. And that's fine. The attitude is…smug.

TRIP. Ouch.

ALLISON. Self-satisfied.

TRIP. Okay.

ALLISON. Vain, even. Vain.

TRIP. Alright, alright. I got it.

ALLISON. Are you?

TRIP. Vain? Maybe a little. But not in a bad way…

ALLISON. What's not a bad way?

TRIP. I'm neat. I always smell nice.

ALLISON. Well, that's a pro.

TRIP. It is.

ALLISON. I know, trust me. And you're not lost, I don't think, which is a big Pro. You might be a little... straightforward for me. A little...uncomplicated. And that's a Con.

TRIP. Uncomplicated is a Con?

ALLISON. Bland. I'm drawn to...depth. Complexity.

TRIP. You're drawn to guys who are crazy?

ALLISON. Crazy, no. Complex, yes.

TRIP. Which are you? Crazy or complex?

ALLISON. What do you think?

TRIP. I'd rather not say.

ALLISON. Then why have dinner with me? If you think I'm crazy?

TRIP. I'm learning. *(pause)* Are you Catholic?

ALLISON. No. Why do you ask?

TRIP. You're wearing a medal. Who is that? Jude?

ALLISON. Lost causes? No. God.

TRIP. Sorry.

ALLISON. It's St. Anthony.

TRIP. St. Anthony?

ALLISON. Domestic animals. Pets. So.

TRIP. That's my name. My real name. Anthony.

ALLISON. Oh.

TRIP. Trip is a nickname.

ALLISON. Right.

TRIP. My real name is Anthony. It's also my Dad's real name, and his Dad's name. I'm Trip, like triple.

ALLISON. Hm.

TRIP. He's also the patron saint of barren women, basket makers, butchers, grave diggers, lost objects, the poor...and excema. Skin disease.

ALLISON. All the same Anthony?

TRIP. Maybe not.

ALLISON. Because I think Rita's the patron saint of barren women.

TRIP. Really.

ALLISON. My sister couldn't conceive.

TRIP. Yeah, I don't know why a man would get to be patron saint of barren women.

ALLISON. It seems inappropriate.

TRIP. But it is the church. How do you know so much about the saints?

ALLISON. I considered converting. Once.

TRIP. Really?

ALLISON. I was raised very...irreligiously, scientifically almost. When I was a teenager...I felt like there had to be something else. Something more than what my parents were. I think I was drawn to Catholicism because right away, it gives you a perfect Father and a nurturing Mother.

TRIP. Hm. So why didn't you? Convert?

ALLISON. You know, to tell you the truth, I did. But then, later, it scared me, the dogma. I guess that's when I became a real Catholic, when I started hating it. So, I never told anyone. I mean, hardly anyone knows.

TRIP. God knows.

ALLISON. God and now you.

TRIP. A Catholic girl.

ALLISON. Well, sort of. What?

TRIP. No, it's funny. It's just – I mean, not that I'm jumping the gun and of course I'll marry whoever I want, but it would just be, you know, better if she were Catholic.

ALLISON. Yeah, well.

TRIP. And it's funny how you're wearing a medal with my name.

ALLISON. Hm. *(pause)* Oh look, there's Cat.

TRIP. Where?

ALLISON. She darted to the box. She's happy because it's clean for once in her life.

TRIP. It's clean a lot.

ALLISON. Mm hm.

TRIP. She went back under the bed.

ALLISON. *(calling)* Cat, here Cat. Caaaat. *(pause)* Hm. Usually, they come when I call them.

TRIP. Cats? She's not a dog, you know.

ALLISON. Is it possible she could be deaf?

TRIP. No. *(pause)* Her name's not really Cat.

ALLISON. What is it?

TRIP. …Pussy.

ALLISON. Pussy.

TRIP. Pussy Cat.

ALLISON. Ah.

TRIP. I thought you might be offended.

ALLISON. But you told me anyway.

TRIP. Earlier, I thought you might be offended.

ALLISON. I'm offended now.

TRIP. Are you?

ALLISON. No. But it's definitely a Con.

TRIP. What would a Pro be? A Pro name for the cat? Fluffy?

ALLISON. No. That cat looks like a Selma to me. An Esther.

TRIP. An old lady?

ALLISON. Yes. She looks like a wise old gal.

TRIP. She's only two.

ALLISON. But she looks like a wise old gal. *(She sips, upset.)* I feel you should change her name.

TRIP. You do?

ALLISON. It's demeaning. No wonder she pees on your bed.

TRIP. I think she likes it. She likes her name.

ALLISON. I'm sorry. It's inappropriate for me to name your cat.

TRIP. So, what are my Pros? Energy and shirt?

ALLISON. Energy, I don't know anymore.

TRIP. Wow. I'm coasting on the shirt, right now.

ALLISON. And you seem to listen. Which is a big Pro. A double pro.

TRIP. Okay. I'm coming back.

ALLISON. What about me? What are my Pros and Cons?

TRIP. Guys don't do that. We take in the whole…zeitgeist.

ALLISON. I don't think that's the right way to use zeitgeist.

TRIP. What do I mean? Enchilada?

ALLISON. Gestalt?

TRIP. Gestalt.

ALLISON. How is my gestalt?

TRIP. Unusual.

ALLISON. Is that good or bad?

TRIP. I don't know. But it's having a good effect on me.

ALLISON. I don't think of myself as unusual. I think of myself as very…standard.

TRIP. You're not. You're really smart and kind of aggressive –

ALLISON. No.

TRIP. Yeah. But you're also…soft. You're very sexy, and you're very uptight. Which makes it hard to figure out the message.

ALLISON. I don't know whether to be flattered or enraged.

(He leans in and kisses her. She responds. It's a hungry kiss for them both.)

Wow.

TRIP. I wasn't sure if you wanted me to do that.

ALLISON. I wasn't exactly thinking about it right then.

TRIP. Sorry. Was that too fast?

ALLISON. I don't know. No.

TRIP. I just…you're very sexy.

ALLISON. And uptight?

TRIP. Yeah, but that's just the veneer, I think.

(He kisses her again. It's really steamy.)

ALLISON. Whoa.

TRIP. Yeah.

ALLISON. Should we go see if we can get the cat to come out?

TRIP. Really?

ALLISON. I didn't mean – that's not what I meant.

TRIP. I know, you want to see the cat.

(He kisses her and pulls her toward the bed.)

ALLISON. Hey, where are we going?

TRIP. We're looking for the cat.

(Still kissing her. The following dialogue happens as necks are kissed, shirts are explored, etc.)

ALLISON. I hope you don't think we're going to be sleeping together tonight.

TRIP. Why would I think that?

ALLISON. I just want to make sure there's no confusion.

TRIP. Okay thanks. *(more making out)* But you should make sure your body knows that.

ALLISON. My body's not in charge here.

TRIP. Maybe it should be, once in a while.

ALLISON. Trust me, it has been.

TRIP. I think your head needs a night off.

ALLISON. I think that sounds very…psychotic.

TRIP. I mean it must get tired.

ALLISON. It does.

(She gasps with pleasure.)

TRIP. See?

ALLISON. But I don't want that to be what this is.

TRIP. I know. It's not.

ALLISON. What is it?

TRIP. It's everything. Can't you tell?

ALLISON. …I don't know.

TRIP. I can tell.

ALLISON. …Really…?

(LIGHTS FADE)

Qualification #1

(**GINA** *sits in a chair.*)

GINA. I always pretty much sexualized things. It's always been a way to feel...alive, you know...real, I guess. But it wasn't real. Because I wasn't really there, it turns out. I was using it to get high, you know? I needed the excitement. The sense of possibility. I never thought about marriage and kids. It was like, why disappoint a whole new round of people, you know? But then I met Paul and it was like looking into a mirror and seeing a man. Like this is finally the Love thing everyone talks about. And I'm so not religious, but it almost felt like we'd been living in sin all our lives before we met. Like it was a totally carnal life. Before we met. And in the beginning, between us, even – the passion was a very animal kind of hunger. We were both sexual in that way...it was the most important thing. It was the only way we could feel anything...connect. But we were so much the same, and so we could see how this life, this constant need for some new conquest was just killing us. We were exhausted from the perpetual... hunger. We knew we had to help each other change. It was like we made a pact to escape Sodom together. And we did. For a while. And then he looked back. He looked back.

Scene Two

*(In her kitchen, **RACHELLE** is hunched over her legs, grabbing her thighs and weeping. **BERT** comes in behind her unseen carrying a baguette.)*

BERT. What are you doing?

*(**RACHELLE** jumps up and pulls down her skirt.)*

RACHELLE. Nothing. What? Nothing.

BERT. Your pantyhose are down.

*(**RACHELLE** pulls up her hose.)*

RACHELLE. I thought you were bowling.

BERT. Enh.

RACHELLE. Enh what? You're supposed to be bowling all day.

BERT. What were you doing?

RACHELLE. Nothing. Emoting.

BERT. Were you having a little fun with yourself?

RACHELLE. What? NO! Jesus, Bert. Jesus.

BERT. You looked kinda guilty.

RACHELLE. Talk about guilty, what are you? Coming home with a loaf of bread you're supposed to be bowling – it's the finals, I thought.

BERT. The bowl-offs.

RACHELLE. Final. Bowl-off. Whatever. You're supposed to be there.

*(**BERT** slices bread.)*

RACHELLE. You're making a sandwich? What do you need the whole loaf?

BERT. I'm doing – I'm making an hors d'ouevre.

RACHELLE. An hors d'ouevre?

BERT. A...crostini, or something,

RACHELLE. What happened?

BERT. Why should I tell you when you don't tell me?

RACHELLE. Fine, then. What do I care? There's no tomato.

BERT. I'll make do.

   (**BERT** *starts taking things out of the fridge.*)

RACHELLE. He'll make do. Help me Mary. He's making appetizers.

   (**BERT** *opens a jar of pimentos.*)

BERT. What's this green?

RACHELLE. Mold.

BERT. Mold.

RACHELLE. It's old. It's from Theresa's birthday. The grinders.

BERT. What are you keeping five year old peppers around?

RACHELLE. They're pimentos. And forgive me. You could on occasion – if you're going to get offended – you could throw things out too, you know. Now that you're home, on occasion.

BERT. What's that supposed to mean? On occasion?

RACHELLE. Well, I haven't quite figured out your schedule.

BERT. It's an adjustment. Sometimes I need to go out, take a walk. I can't just sit around all day.

RACHELLE. We could take a cruise…?

BERT. On what?

RACHELLE. With our savings. This is what you save for.

BERT. You save for an emergency. I'm boiling some eggs.

RACHELLE. Fine. Be my guest. I'm fascinated.

BERT. What were you going to do today?

RACHELLE. Go shopping, maybe. The gym.

BERT. The gym? What gym?

RACHELLE. The gym down the street.

BERT. Since when do you go to a gym?

RACHELLE. Since I go sign up.

BERT. What's that?

RACHELLE. Nothing. A need to be physical.

BERT. A need to be physical?

RACHELLE. Not like that. Like…healthy. A need to…sweat. To…tone.

BERT. A need to tone?

RACHELLE. Yes. What? It's normal. Most people run around a few times a week. You bowl. Or you did. You used to bowl every Saturday. Now, I don't know, maybe you make crostini on the weekend.

*(Silence. **BERT** arranges slices of bread on a tray.)*

Alright. I'm going to the store. You want tomatoes?

BERT. No. I hate tomatoes.

RACHELLE. Since when?

BERT. Always. They stink from the store. If you don't grow a tomato, it's crap. It's mealy pesticide crap.

RACHELLE. Oh, so now we're an organic farmer? What next? We're gonna get a cow in here for fresh milk?

BERT. No. I just don't like tomatoes from the store.

RACHELLE. So what do you want? Anything?

BERT. It's not like you'll be back in time for my snack.

RACHELLE. Who knew you were coming home for a happy hour?

(She starts to go.)

BERT. You got a hole in those, babe.

RACHELLE. I do?

BERT. *(Pointing to her tights)* Here.

RACHELLE. Oh. Shoot. These are Donna Karen – well, maybe I can…

*(She exits. **BERT** boils eggs. **RACHELLE** returns with nail polish, puts it on her run.)*

BERT. You're going out with that?

RACHELLE. You can't see it under my skirt…can you?

BERT. Why not just change your stockings?

RACHELLE. *(still holding up her skirt)* What do you think?

BERT. What do I – I think you should change your hose.

RACHELLE. What else?

BERT. What else nothing.

RACHELLE. You think I'm…aging?

BERT. Aging? What are you talking? We're all aging.

RACHELLE. So you do?

BERT. You have to be aging Rachelle. It's the human condition.

RACHELLE. But – fast? Too fast?

BERT. Too fast? No, at the same rate as everyone else, I'd say.

RACHELLE. I'm sorry.

BERT. You're – what are you sorry – for aging? It's not your fault, honey bun. That was God's decision.

(**RACHELLE** *cries.*)

What? What?

RACHELLE. For...how I've been.

BERT. Oh. *(pause)* Is it over now?

RACHELLE. No.

BERT. So why bring it up?

RACHELLE. I hate the cold.

BERT. What're ya gonna do.

RACHELLE. I used to dream of moving to Tampa. Now...I couldn't.

BERT. It's not my fault I got laid off –

RACHELLE. No, that's not what I – I can't ever wear shorts again, I'm saying. I can't go to the beach.

BERT. Well, good. Because Tampa's no paradise. Palm Beach, maybe. We'd get you pajamas. Beach pajamas. You'd be fine.

(**RACHELLE** *laughs tearily.*)

RACHELLE. I love you.

BERT. Now you love me.

(**RACHELLE** *goes to hold him.*)

RACHELLE. I do. I do. I'm sorry.

BERT. You wanna maybe...Go lie down a little?

RACHELLE. Oh...no. I mean, we could nap.

BERT. Forget it. I'm sorry I asked.

RACHELLE. Bert, you're burning – Bert – the bread!

> (**BERT** *opens the oven and grabs the baking pan without a rag – he drops it.*)

BERT. OW! FUCK! FUCK!

RACHELLE. Honey? Did you burn it?

BERT. Yes, I fucking – what does it look like?

RACHELLE. Put it in ice! Put it in ice!

BERT. What ice?!

RACHELLE. In the freezer! Oh, honey. Why'd you touch the pan with no mitts on?

BERT. I forgot, what do you think, I did it on purpose?

RACHELLE. You need the mitts.

BERT. Maybe if you kept the mitts near the oven – I wouldn't –

RACHELLE. Here. Here.

> (**RACHELLE** *wraps his hand up in ice.*)

BERT. There was no Bowl-Off.

RACHELLE. There wasn't?

BERT. No.

RACHELLE. Why not?

BERT. We got knocked out two rounds ago.

RACHELLE. …did you forget?

BERT. No.

RACHELLE. Oh.

> (*silence*)

BERT. I don't know what to do with myself anymore.

RACHELLE. You need a hobby.

BERT. It's so hard with so many empty days, Shell.

RACHELLE. Sign up for some classes.

BERT. I went –

RACHELLE. – I don't want to know.

BERT. I have to tell you.

RACHELLE. No you don't. I don't want to know.

BERT. But I stopped, Shell. I stopped before it –

RACHELLE. Alright, then. Good. Wonderful.

BERT. I drove to the bowling alley first, because I thought maybe that's all I need to do. Drive out, and by the time I get there, it'll be over. Then I got to the bowling alley and kept going.

RACHELLE. Please, Bert –

BERT. Then – I don't know how, I'm at the Russian place and I'm asking the guy for a red head. And I get in the booth with her, and I hear the timer go on and I think, "these are the seconds of my life. This is all I have. This is my Saturday afternoon. I'm the one in this room right now." So I get up. I walked out with the timer still going. I came back home, Shelley. I came back home.

RACHELLE. Are you done?

BERT. Yeah, I'm done.

   (silence)

Qualification #2

(BECKY sits in a chair.)

BECKY. The funny thing is, I always thought I had this really
hot body. Like when other women bitched about being
too fat or whatever, I never felt that way. I knew it wasn't
perfect, but I really thought it was nice. I always liked
being naked, you know. I was happy to have sex with
the lights on. Then I started seeing Mitch – my partner, I mean, and he had all these issues with…well, you
know, sex. He couldn't really, sometimes he could, but
most of the time, he couldn't get an erection? And after
it happened a few times he said maybe it was because
I wasn't really his "type" physically. Because I had
such small breasts? And at first I just thought that was
ridiculous, because no one else had ever had a problem with them. Then he said something about how he
didn't usually go for brunettes. By the way, his mother
is this incredibly voluptuous bottle blonde. Fat, really.
She's fat. But anyway, it went on like this. He was "in
love with me" but there just seemed to be something
wrong with the way I looked. So, first, I lightened my
hair. Because you know, at a certain point, who doesn't?
But then I started noticing other women's breasts.
They all looked so much bigger and more luscious
than mine. I couldn't believe I'd never noticed before
how…depleted I was in this area. It seemed like all the
men I'd ever had sex with must have been very nice to
act as though I had a nice body when really, they were
horribly disappointed by my sad little tiny breasts. Well,
I guess it's pretty obvious what I did next. *(She unzips
her sweatshirt. The tight top beneath reveals that she has large
round surgically enhanced breasts.)* And, for a few weeks he
was really into it, but then it just wore off or something.
I used to think there were a million ways to be beautiful, now it seems impossible. And every mark, every
scar or mole on my body is like…a betrayal. Like that's
the thing that made this happen to me. The reason I
can't be happy. I used to be the only woman I knew
who loved her body. Now, I'm just like everyone else.

Scene Three

(TRIP and ALLISON make out in the living room.)

TRIP. Oh my God, you're so…you're so.

ALLISON. So what?

TRIP. So…perfect.

ALLISON. You are.

TRIP. Shh.

ALLISON. You are.

(She tears up a little.)

TRIP. What?

ALLISON. I just. I can't believe it.

TRIP. It's okay.

ALLISON. No, I mean…this. You know, finally.

TRIP. Yeah. I know. I know.

ALLISON. I just feel so…you know.

TRIP. I know. I was scared it would never happen.

ALLISON. Me too! Me too! I was really ready to give up…

TRIP. I think this is it for me.

(They kiss passionately.)

ALLISON. It does. It feels so…right. God, it's such a relief.

TRIP. I knew as soon as you walked in.

ALLISON. You did?

TRIP. Didn't you? When you had my name around your neck?

(He peels off her clothes.)

ALLISON. I can't tell anymore. My first impressions are so wrong, usually.

TRIP. You thought I was an asshole.

(He kisses down her body.)

ALLISON. No, I didn't. Oh. My god.

TRIP. Didn't you?

ALLISON. *(reacting physically)* Oooh. I was drawn to you.

   (He gets on top of her.)

TRIP. You didn't show it.

ALLISON. Well you figured it out.

TRIP. I took a gamble.

   (He starts to enter her.)

ALLISON. Mmmm.

   (A moment as he tries to keep the momentum going but can't. Several tries. Then he suddenly stops.)

   What?

TRIP. I don't know.

ALLISON. Is…? Are you okay?

TRIP. …yeah…I don't know.

ALLISON. What is it? What's the matter?

TRIP. I'm just, you know…not…I don't know what's going on.

ALLISON. Hm.

TRIP. It's just…really weird.

ALLISON. It happens.

TRIP. Not to me.

ALLISON. Oh.

TRIP. I mean, sorry. I don't mean to sound…but this really isn't…familiar to me.

ALLISON. Well, it's not exactly familiar to me either.

TRIP. Hm.

ALLISON. Maybe you're just nervous.

TRIP. But why?

ALLISON. Well, because of the feelings.

TRIP. What feelings?

ALLISON. You said you were feeling, you know…some very positive, you know, feelings…

TRIP. Oh, right.

ALLISON. So that can make someone feel…nervous, don't you think?

TRIP. What if I start pissing all over the bed?

ALLISON. Excuse me?

TRIP. That was just a joke.

ALLISON. Right. I guess I'd have to make sure you had a tidy box.

(pause)

TRIP. Did you ever…shave?

ALLISON. What?

TRIP. Did you ever shave down there?

ALLISON. You mean, wax?

TRIP. I guess. I don't know how they do it.

ALLISON. I wax, you know, the edges. Why, does it look… unruly?

TRIP. No. I meant, like, you know…more.

ALLISON. Like, all?

TRIP. Not all…

ALLISON. Because I think that's really just not nice.

TRIP. But like, the sides…

ALLISON. The sides? You mean the landing strip thing?

TRIP. No, like long on top, short on the sides. Like a good haircut.

ALLISON. Hm.

TRIP. Like the lips are clean.

ALLISON. Eiew. *(pause)* You know, I saw this woman at the gym who had like a little…puff down there, like the tiniest little piece of fluff. I mean, I didn't want to stare. But it was horrifying! I thought she'd had chemotherapy or something.

TRIP. I don't think so. It's pretty common. Now.

ALLISON. Well I just can't go on, then. If that's what it's come to. That little puff. Where's the dignity?

TRIP. Yeah. It's okay. It doesn't matter.

(They lay there, silent.)

ALLISON. That's not why…?

TRIP. This? Oh no. *(pause)* I don't think so.

ALLISON. Okay. Well, that's good.

(He kisses her half-heartedly. She holds his face, trying to reach him. He pulls away.)

TRIP. I feel like, maybe, it's that I'm not attracted to you.

ALLISON. What?

TRIP. Yeah, that's what it feels like.

ALLISON. Are you kidding?

TRIP. No. I know, it's really weird…

ALLISON. You just said I was perfect.

TRIP. I know. But I just don't feel that…thing, you know.

ALLISON. Since when?

TRIP. I don't know. Maybe…from the beginning.

ALLISON. It can't have been from the beginning! You were so…eager.

TRIP. Yeah, but…I don't know. It's never been really.. you know…. Hot. For me.

ALLISON. I just…I'm just very confused. Why would you even…start all this, if you weren't…?

TRIP. I really like you. I just liked you so much. I didn't want to see it.

ALLISON. But…are you saying you don't think…I'm attractive?

TRIP. No, I can see that you're…attractive. I just don't feel – sexually – attracted to you.

ALLISON. Oh. Well, then. That's not good.

TRIP. No.

(pause)

ALLISON. So, I guess this isn't going to work out.

TRIP. I don't know…

ALLISON. But you just said.

TRIP. I know, but maybe I'm wrong.

ALLISON. What would it be? If you were wrong?

TRIP. I don't know. I just want to be wrong. You know, I've been dating for so long…. I haven't liked someone this much since…I don't even know. High school, really.

ALLISON. Then, how can you not…? I mean, usually men find me very…appealing.

TRIP. I know. You're perfect. You are. In every other way.

ALLISON. It's odd. This just coming out of nowhere. Are you sure it's not just…fear?

TRIP. It could be. Maybe it is.

ALLISON. I really think it might be.

TRIP. Let's not talk about it for a while.

(long pause)

ALLISON. How was your day?

TRIP. Okay. How was yours?

ALLISON. Okay. I leash broke a schnauzer.

(long pause)

TRIP. I really like you.

ALLISON. Thanks.

TRIP. I mean, I like how I feel with you.

ALLISON. How do you feel with me?

TRIP. I don't know. Like there's hope.

ALLISON. That's so nice. *(pause)* I think it's because of the feelings. I do.

TRIP. Yeah. Maybe.

ALLISON. But was I wrong? In the beginning? That first night? When it seemed like you were so…you know… passionate, sort of? That was all…intellectual?

TRIP. No, you're right. The first night it was. It was hot.

ALLISON. Okay, that's what I thought. So…?

TRIP. The first date, it's something else…it's the newness, the challenge. And you're such a good girl. It was such a challenge.

ALLISON. That's all?

TRIP. And I liked you, as a person. That's what I'm saying.

ALLISON. I just think if you like someone…?

TRIP. I know. It should.

ALLISON. But…?

TRIP. It doesn't.

   (*silence*)

ALLISON. And you know, I'm not that good a girl.

TRIP. Yes, you are. I can tell.

ALLISON. I slept with you on the first date.

TRIP. I'm very persuasive.

ALLISON. Yeah, but it's not like I never do that.

TRIP. You acted like you don't.

ALLISON. I was trying to turn over a new leaf. (*She sighs.*)
   Why doesn't she ever come out from under the bed?

TRIP. You tell me.

   (**ALLISON** *stares under the bed.*)

ALLISON. She's not there.

TRIP. She's not?

ALLISON. Is she…? Where is she?

TRIP. In the closet, I guess.

   (**ALLISON** *looks in the closet.*)

ALLISON. Kitty…Pussy? (*Uch.*) She's not here.

TRIP. Well, she's got to be somewhere.

ALLISON. But when did you see her last?

   (**ALLISON** *opens the cabinet.* **TRIP** *tries to stop her.*)

TRIP. She's not –

   (**ALLISON** *sees shelves of videos and DVDs.*)

ALLISON. Wow. You have a lot of movies…

   (*She pulls out a porn DVD.*)

   Well, this is interesting.

TRIP. Are you into it?

ALLISON. I don't know. I could be. Are you?

TRIP. I'm asking you.

ALLISON. Well, it's never done that much for me. But, I
   don't know. If you're into it…

TRIP. You want to watch one?

ALLISON. Whoa. Are they all…?

TRIP. Yeah. It's just like a collection, from when I was a kid.

ALLISON. Oh. Wow. That's a lot of porn.

TRIP. It's just a collection. Like baseball cards.

ALLISON. Hm. How do you choose?

TRIP. It's just like any other movie. You know, what you're in the mood for.

(He goes to the DVD player, and ejects the DVD that's in there. **ALLISON** *reaches for the DVD.)*

ALLISON. Let's see that one.

TRIP. Nah. That one won't be good for you –

ALLISON. I want to see the last one you watched. I mean, it doesn't really matter if you know the ending, does it?

TRIP. *(laughs nervously)* No.

*(***ALLISON** *puts the DVD into the DVD player. A guy half dressed as a cop handcuffs a voluptuous woman. Her pubic hair is waxed into a tiny v.)*

ALLISON. Oh, that's what you meant.

TRIP. Hunh?

ALLISON. The way she's waxed.

TRIP. Yeah, that's pretty much it.

ALLISON. Pretty much?

TRIP. No, that's it.

(They watch.)

ALLISON. God, I know it's supposed to be such a hot thing, watching porn, but I just don't get it, really.

TRIP. It's just fantasy.

ALLISON. But I feel like the fantasies I make up are so much more interesting.

TRIP. Men are more visual.

ALLISON. But women are into it, too, aren't they?

TRIP. Some.

ALLISON. I don't get it.

(*She turns it off.*)

I'm sorry. It's just…depressing, sort of.

TRIP. Are you thinking I'm some kind of freak?

ALLISON. No. I thought you were thinking I was.

TRIP. No, I mean, it's a little much. I know.

ALLISON. I don't know. People have orgies.

TRIP. What do you mean?

ALLISON. Just…you know, it's a very sexual time, a…liberated time. High school girls are all doling out the oral sex to anyone who asks…. Girls Gone Wild. Girls have gone wild.

TRIP. So?

ALLISON. So, you know, we've evolved to that point. Monogamy is retro. Intimacy is a thing of the past.

TRIP. I don't think that. I think people should get married and be faithful. Porn just helps you do that.

ALLISON. Has it helped you do that?

TRIP. Not yet. But it will. When I do. I think.

ALLISON. Mm…

TRIP. What?

ALLISON. Nothing. (*pause*) You have such a beautiful house.

TRIP. I think I spend too much time alone.

ALLISON. How much time do you spend alone?

TRIP. It's been years since I had someone…I liked who was…close to me.

ALLISON. Do you think you might have some kind of madonna/whore thing?

TRIP. You think there's something really wrong about my collection.

ALLISON. I didn't say that.

TRIP. But you feel it.

ALLISON. But maybe that's my problem.

TRIP. I don't think so.

ALLISON. Why not?

TRIP. I just. I think, maybe, I depend on it…a little too much.

ALLISON. How much do you depend on it?

TRIP. Just…more than I should, maybe.

ALLISON. Mm hm. *(pause)* Maybe you should throw it out.

TRIP. Maybe.

ALLISON. I'll help you throw it out.

TRIP. Right now?

ALLISON. Where do you keep your garbage bags – under the sink?

(She heads into the kitchen.)

TRIP. Wait, I don't know if I want to do this right this second –

ALLISON. *(calling)* There's no time like the present!

TRIP. I know, but –

*(**ALLISON** appears holding some garbage bags.)*

ALLISON. Didn't you just say there was something wrong about it?

TRIP. Well, yeah, but –

ALLISON. So?

TRIP. I know, but it's just like years in there, and a lot of those you can't get anywhere in the world now, they're valuable.

ALLISON. So you want to sell them?

TRIP. Well, yeah, I don't think they should be destroyed. They're like artifacts. Some of these are even Betamax!

ALLISON. We'll sell them on E-bay.

TRIP. Oh come on, we'd have to catalogue them all –

ALLISON. Why don't you type up the list and I'll take it from there.

TRIP. Okay.

ALLISON. Where's your computer?

TRIP. We don't have to do this now.

ALLISON. I'd like to just get it out of the way. Then I can take the tapes when I leave.

TRIP. Why are you so into this?

ALLISON. I think it will help you. I want to help you.

TRIP. Why?

ALLISON. I think this could be the reason, for, you know...

TRIP. I really don't think so.

ALLISON. I really do.

TRIP. But then you're saying there is something...like, wrong with me.

ALLISON. Nothing can't be fixed with behavior modification.

TRIP. You can't even get my cat out from under the bed.

ALLISON. She's not under the bed, she's in your linens. Above the dryer.

TRIP. You saw her.

ALLISON. Yes, we just had a moment. Has she gone outside the box? Since we met?

TRIP. No.

ALLISON. See.

(**ALLISON** *starts pulling tapes and DVDs off the shelves.*)

(*LIGHTS FADE*)

Qualification #3

*(**GRETCHEN** sits in a chair.)*

GRETCHEN. Okay, um. Woah. This is weird. I'm not that
– I don't like talking that much. About myself or
whatever. I don't know if this is, okay to say this, or
whatever, but, I met my husband at a club where I was
dancing. I was an exotic dancer. That's not my thing
anymore, since we met. He was like "that's it for that"
you know. I liked it, actually. The money's incredible,
compared to waiting tables and whatever other forms
of slavery. Telemarketing. I did that once, I would sell
all these office supply packages and come the next
day, the manager's like "That buyer backed out. No
commission for you." Right. Backed out my ass maybe.
So, I don't know, I hope none of you are like "she's
the enemy." I don't do it anymore. *(She looks around,
then continues.)* I'm all little homemaker now. But it's
not like I didn't know my husband was into porn. That
was my scene. And he's a sexual guy. I mean, I always
went out with guys who had pretty big sex drives. But
his is like, you know, major. Like he has to do it pretty
much a few times a day. But I've got kids to take care
of now. I just don't have time for all that. I've got to
make dinner, you know? But I don't want him to feel
like he has to go somewhere else. So I made up these
rules like he can do porn if I'm out of town, if I'm
on my period, or pregnant, obviously, or if we're in a
fight. But never when the kids are around. He's a good
dad. He is. I don't even have to work anymore. I get to
hang out with my kids and be this mom I never had,
which is like my idea of heaven. We live in Pelham
– it's kind of like a fairy tale, you know? Except he
breaks the rules all the time. They're just such basic
rules. Like what if my daughter wanted to check her
e-mail and caught him doing his thing – we share the
computer. It's not like I think it's so bad, I just don't
want her seeing that.

Scene Four

(RACHELLE sits in the dark kitchen with piles of receipts on the table. TRIP enters.)

TRIP. Mom?

(RACHELLE vaguely raises a hand.)

You doing taxes?

(He opens the refrigerator and gets out a Coke.)

You're sitting in the dark.

(He turns on the light.)

I thought you were making dinner.

RACHELLE. I'm sorry.

TRIP. What's the matter. You sick?

(Flushed, RACHELLE pats her face with a dish rag.)

What's wrong? You got a fever?

(He puts his hand on her forehead. She clutches it.)

You're hot. What Mom?

RACHELLE. It's nice. Your hand. So cool.

TRIP. What's going on here?

RACHELLE. Nothing. I'm just happy you came.

TRIP. You knew I was coming. We're gonna have dinner, I thought. Where's Dad?

RACHELLE. He has bowling.

TRIP. On Sunday?

RACHELLE. It's some kind of tournament.

TRIP. Oh. Should we go?

RACHELLE. Not tonight.

(TRIP picks up a receipt.)

TRIP. The Ritz-Carlton? When'd you go to the Ritz-Carlton?

RACHELLE. I didn't.

(pause)

TRIP. Dad went without you?

(**RACHELLE** *starts piling up the receipts.*)

Mom? You wanna tell me what's going on?

RACHELLE. I should…I was going to make dinner.

TRIP. Don't worry about dinner.

RACHELLE. I was going to make your veal piccata.

TRIP. Let me take you out for dinner.

RACHELLE. Look at this handsome young man, I got here.

TRIP. I'll treat you someplace nice.

RACHELLE. I can't go out looking like this.

TRIP. Go get yourself gussied up. I can wait.

RACHELLE. Am I an ugly old woman?

TRIP. What are you talking about? You're gorgeous. You're beautiful. All my friends usta have the hots for you.

RACHELLE. Then.

TRIP. Still, they do.

RACHELLE. They do not. *(pause)* Who?

TRIP. They do. Mikey Felcher.

RACHELLE. Stop. What's he doing now?

TRIP. He's a big contractor out on the Island. You remember. He does the malls.

RACHELLE. Married?

TRIP. Oh yeah. Twice.

RACHELLE. Twice already. And you not even. Gorgeous boy like you.

TRIP. *(smiling)* Yeah, well.

RACHELLE. What? 'Dya meet someone?

TRIP. I think maybe, yeah. I think maybe I did.

RACHELLE. You met someone?

TRIP. Ma, I meet people every day. It's not like I'm not trying. I go on dates all the time.

RACHELLE. Dates.

TRIP. Because I'm looking! I'm trying. You think I don't want to make you happy?

RACHELLE. Me? It's not for me. It's for you. I just don't want you to end up like your brother dragging home bimbos from the bar. They steal from him now, you know.

TRIP. I know, you told me.

RACHELLE. One of 'em walked off with his wallet.

TRIP. I know –

RACHELLE. This is the one he said he wanted to marry.

TRIP. I know. We met her.

RACHELLE. Easter lunch, I swear to Mary.

TRIP. I thought she was a nice person.

RACHELLE. She was drunk. Good riddance. So, are you going to tell me?

TRIP. I was. But you wanted to go off on Johnny.

RACHELLE. I'm not going off, I'm being realistic.

TRIP. Well, do you want to hear this or not?

RACHELLE. First, where did you meet her?

TRIP. You can't let me tell it?

RACHELLE. Oh no. It's not good?

TRIP. I met her at my apartment.

RACHELLE. She's selling door to door? She's not with some environment group. Because I think those people are very pushy.

TRIP. She works with animals. She's a behaviorist. She came over to look at the cat.

RACHELLE. Uch. That cat. Why you don't just put the cat out of its misery, I'll never know. Three thousand dollar couch she goes on. She's a vet?

TRIP. She's a behaviorist. Like a shrink for pets.

RACHELLE. Thousands of dollars of furniture that cat ruins and now we're spending money so the cat can talk about her childhood.

TRIP. Anyway, Allison cured the cat.

RACHELLE. Allison. Is she…? What is she?

TRIP. She's Catholic. As if anyone cares about that anymore.

RACHELLE. I care.

TRIP. Anyone but you.

RACHELLE. I'm not the only one. This whole neighborhood cares.

TRIP. Okay, well good. Go tell everyone.

RACHELLE. Who does she look like?

TRIP. Who? Like herself.

RACHELLE. I mean, like who would play her in the movie?

TRIP. I don't know…Liza Flynn Boyle, maybe?

RACHELLE. Lara Flynn Boyle? So she's cold?

TRIP. No. It's just who came to mind. You'll meet her, alright?

RACHELLE. Is she older than you?

TRIP. No.

RACHELLE. Because Lara Flynn Boyle must be in her midforties by now.

TRIP. Will you stop with the Lara Flynn Boyle already?

RACHELLE. When did all this happen?

TRIP. A couple of months.

RACHELLE. A couple of months already and now you tell me?

TRIP. I wanted to wait 'til I knew it was something special.

(RACHELLE *sighs, miserable.*)

What's the matter? You're not happy? I thought this was going to be the greatest day of your life.

RACHELLE. I want it all to go better for you than it did for me.

TRIP. It went alright for you, Mom.

RACHELLE. Well, I got you. I got you.

(Pause. **RACHELLE** *lapses into herself.* **TRIP** *picks up a receipt.*)

TRIP. Why would he do this?

RACHELLE. I don't know. I thought he was too old for all this now.

TRIP. But be so obvious like this.

RACHELLE. He hates having secrets from me.

TRIP. So why does he?

RACHELLE. He wants me to know. He comes home late, he smells of her, and it's the same smell, not like before, when it was different smells, I never had to remember them. Now, it's a smell I know, like a person coming home in his pockets.

TRIP. Oh, Ma. I'm sorry. You want me to talk to him?

RACHELLE. I shouldna never told you. Please, forget I told you.

TRIP. How'm I going to forget you looking like this? Over and over the bastard does this to you. And you let him, Ma. Why?

RACHELLE. You don't know what marriage is like.

TRIP. It's a prison you lock yourself into? That's what everybody gets so excited about?

RACHELLE. It's…an understanding. An ongoing understanding.

TRIP. What'd you get that out of some book? Offa some talk show? You're dying in this. People don't put up with this shit anymore. Even the Pope would beg you to get the hell out of this.

RACHELLE. No, he knows you don't get married to be happy. *(pause)* You get married to learn compassion.

TRIP. Yeah, well someone should tell Dad that.

RACHELLE. He tries, sweetie. He tries.

TRIP. I don't see it.

RACHELLE. You don't know how hard it is to be a weak man. To never make anything of yourself.

TRIP. Whose fault is that, he never made anything of himself?

RACHELLE. He never had the confidence you have.

TRIP. Come on, I'm taking you to Ennio's.

(**RACHELLE** *reaches for* **TRIP** *and clings to him.*)

RACHELLE. I thank God for you. I thank God for you.

TRIP. Come on, we're going out on the town, alright?

(He pulls her out of her chair. She clings to him, shaking.)

We're going out on the town.

(LIGHTS FADE)

Qualification #4

(**PAMELA** *lowers herself into a chair.*)

PAMELA. I'm still in shock. This just happened a few months ago. I still don't even know what to do. I'm supposed to have this baby in six weeks. Every day I just get more pregnant and I don't even know what my life is anymore. Oh Lord, I'm babbling. The thing is, I don't know if this is true for the rest of you? But we were really happy. We met through our church! Maybe I should have known...when he wanted to wait...to be intimate until we got married, but I thought, you know it was sweet and that he was very... religious. And we both wanted to start a family right away. But then, that part of things was...never...quite right. Okay. Okay. *(She tries to calm herself)* I just have to say it. I was on his computer, looking to see if a check had cleared – he had the program for all that, and they were calling from some company. It was a check I wrote – I wasn't looking for something, just this check. There were all these...pictures. I can't say anything more about them. But he's, oh Lord. He's a doctor. He works with children…. What could I do? With a baby coming. I couldn't let him stay here. I couldn't tell my parents. They don't understand what's happening, but I don't want him to go to – I don't want to ruin his life. If you knew him – he's the last person anyone would ever…. And now, I'm in this perfect house we bought in the best school district. And everything in it is new. Every single piece of furniture is something we chose together, nothing from my life before, even. And it's like these lamps are just tormenting me, the couch, the bed. He's in all of it. I thought about moving in with my sister, but that's just crazy. I don't even have a job. I was just a receptionist. I just wanted to be a mom. And the nursery is all set up, he put together the crib. He made all the little stencils...the yellow ducks…. But part of me feels like, how can I put the baby in there? And part of me thinks I'll just wake

up and everything will be back like it was. I'll just…
find the missing check. And explain to the company:
we paid that bill. Everything is fine. Does this sound
crazy? Do I sound crazy? *(pause)* Oh right, you're not
supposed to say anything.

Scene Five

(TRIP leads ALLISON into his living room. She is carry-
ing several books.)

ALLISON. So, I did some research.

TRIP. Uh, okay....

ALLISON. I want to ask you some questions, do you mind?
It's like a quiz.

TRIP. Okay.

(She sits down, starts reading, pen poised.)

ALLISON. "Were you sexually abused as a child or ado-
lescent?"

TRIP. Excuse me?

ALLISON. You don't have to tell me, but maybe you could
make a mental note?

TRIP. I wasn't.

ALLISON. Are you sure?

TRIP. How could I not be sure?

ALLISON. Some people block out memories from their
childhoods, traumatic memories, I mean.

TRIP. I don't think I did. *(pause)* Who would have abused
me?

ALLISON. "A parent, relative, family friend, teacher or other
caretaker?" A stranger? Though that's not as common.
Sadly.

TRIP. That is sad.

ALLISON. So, for now, we'll say "no." "Have you subscribed
to or regularly purchased sexually explicit magazines?"
Well, we know the answer to that, right?

(She puts a check on her list.)

"Did your parents have trouble with sexual behavior?"

TRIP. What does that mean?

ALLISON. What does it mean to you?

TRIP. I don't know, that's why I'm asking you.

ALLISON. I think it means, like, were they repressed, or really uptight about sexuality when you were growing up.

TRIP. Hm. Aren't all parents?

ALLISON. I'll take that as a "yes." "Do you often find yourself preoccupied with sexual thoughts?"

TRIP. What's often?

ALLISON. Okay. *(She puts down a check.)* "Do you feel that your sexual behavior is not normal?" Well, we know that's a "yes."

TRIP. We do?

ALLISON. You said.

TRIP. Okay, put a yes.

ALLISON. I did. "Does your spouse (or significant other) ever worry or complain about your sexual behavior?" That's an "N/A."

TRIP. Do you?

ALLISON. I'm not exactly your significant other.

TRIP. Yes, you are.

ALLISON. I am?

TRIP. Don't you feel like you are?

ALLISON. I don't know…maybe. A little.

TRIP. So, that would be a "yes."

ALLISON. I guess so. *(reading)* "Do you have trouble stopping your sexual behavior when you know it is inappropriate?"

TRIP. Inappropriate? According to who?

ALLISON. According to you.

TRIP. Well then, no. I don't think my sexual behavior is inappropriate.

ALLISON. What about the collection?

TRIP. That's not behavior.

ALLISON. What did you do with the collection? Didn't you behave in some way, with the collection?

TRIP. Okay, but that's appropriate. That's appropriate behavior for that situation.

ALLISON. Fine. You can wrestle with that one privately. "Do you ever feel bad about your sexual behavior?"

TRIP. I guess so. I guess I do. I did.

ALLISON. "Has your sexual behavior ever created problems for you or your family?" That's a "yes."

TRIP. It is?

ALLISON. Well, this thing with me.

TRIP. What thing with you?

ALLISON. Your impotence.

TRIP. I'm not impotent. I just don't find you sexually attractive.

ALLISON. I wish you wouldn't put it that way.

TRIP. How should I put it?

ALLISON. You could put it in terms of your madonna/whore problem.

TRIP. I never said I had a madonna/whore problem.

ALLISON. Trip. *(pause)* "Have you ever sought help for sexual behavior that you did not like?"

TRIP. I didn't seek it, but I seem to have gotten it.

ALLISON. "Have you ever worried about people finding out about your sexual activities?"

TRIP. Did you fill this out already?

ALLISON. Just in pencil. I was guessing.

TRIP. So, what'd you put for that?

ALLISON. Well, obviously, it's a "yes." I saw your face when I opened the cabinet.

TRIP. Do you want a drink?

ALLISON. Yes, I'd love some white wine.

(He gets up to get it.)

"Has anyone been hurt emotionally because of your sexual behavior?"

TRIP. It sounds like the same question over and over again.

ALLISON. I know, but it's not. *(She checks "yes.")* "Are any of your sexual activities against the law?"

TRIP. Probably, in this country.

ALLISON. You find the laws in this country restrictive?

TRIP. It was a joke. About the current climate.

ALLISON. Okay. Are they? Against the law?

TRIP. I really don't think so.

ALLISON. I didn't either. I had a "no" there.

TRIP. Thanks.

ALLISON. "Have you made efforts to quit a type of sexual behavior and failed?"

TRIP. No.

ALLISON. Really. Hm. *(She checks "no.")* "Do you have to hide some aspects of your sexual behavior from others?"

TRIP. That's definitely the same as –

ALLISON. You're right. So, it's just a "yes." "Have you attempted to stop some parts of your sexual activities?"

TRIP. That one too.

ALLISON. "Yes." "Have you ever felt degraded by your sexual behavior?"

TRIP. No!

ALLISON. "Has sex been a way for you to escape your problems?"

TRIP. Sometimes. But that's just human.

ALLISON. No one's judging you. It's just a "yes." "When you have sex, do you feel depressed afterward?

TRIP. No. I don't know. Maybe.

ALLISON. I'll put a half on that one.

TRIP. You can do halves? Then I want to go back over a few of these.

ALLISON. "Have you been sexual with minors?"

TRIP. When I was a minor.

ALLISON. So, "yes."

TRIP. No. That is not a "yes." That's a "no."

ALLISON. *(erasing)* "Do you feel controlled by your sexual desire?"

TRIP. No.

ALLISON. "Do you ever think that your sexual desire is stronger than you are?"

TRIP. Ever?

ALLISON. "Yes."

(She starts adding up the score.)

TRIP. So, how'd I do?

ALLISON. Well, they say "if you answer yes to five or more, then you may have a serious problem; ten or more, then you should seek help."

TRIP. How many "Yeses" did I have?

ALLISON. Thirteen and a half. Or fifteen, including the debateable ones.

TRIP. Hm.

ALLISON. They "suggest you seek out the help of a professional who has an understanding of addiction and that you look into sexual recovery groups in your area."

TRIP. Wait. What?

ALLISON. They "suggest you seek out the help of a professional who has an understanding of addiction – "

TRIP. Addiction?

ALLISON. Have you heard of sexual addiction?

TRIP. Yeah, like a joke.

ALLISON. It's a real thing. It's the same as alcoholism.

TRIP. For perverts maybe. Or actors.

ALLISON. No, it's just regular people. You get addicted to the serotonin rush you get from orgasm, or from sexual intrigue. There are a number of manifestations, but a compulsive use of pornography is very common. They think the problem is far more widespread than anyone knows because it's only been about twenty-five years they've known it was a disease –

TRIP. That's such bullshit. A disease is something wrong in your body.

ALLISON. Well, there is mental illness.

TRIP. Look, I hate to disappoint you, but I think it's kind of a weird theory that I'm some kind of sex addict when the last thing I want to do is have sex with you.

ALLISON. I understand that what I'm saying is threatening. You don't have to agree with me, but I will just say, for the record, that according to what I've read, it's quite common for people with this...condition to have trouble mixing intimacy with sex. They can't make love to their wife, but they can have sex with a stranger or a prostitute.

TRIP. Great, there's your madonna/whore theory.

ALLISON. Yes. Exactly.

TRIP. Okay. Well. I appreciate all the work you've put into this.

ALLISON. It's my pleasure.

(Pause. They stare at each another.)

Are you...how are you?

TRIP. Not so hungry, actually.

ALLISON. Right. Me neither...

(An awkward pause.)

TRIP. So maybe we should take a raincheck...

ALLISON. Oh. Okay...

*(**ALLISON** awkwardly heads to the door.)*

TRIP. Don't forget your books.

ALLISON. Those are for you.

TRIP. I can pick up my own.

ALLISON. Well, until then, why don't you borrow these?

TRIP. That's okay.

*(**ALLISON** hurriedly opens the door to exit.)*

ALLISON. No, really. Bye now!

TRIP. Bye.

*(The door slams. **TRIP** picks up one of the books and reads. After a moment, he starts to cry.)*

(LIGHTS FADE)

Qualification #5

(CLAUDIA sits in her chair.)

CLAUDIA. Okay. I'm Claudia, and I'm pissed off right now.
I'm just coming from a movie with Frank. And he
picks it, of course, since he has to pick every movie
and everything we see on TV. And I guess he thought
it would be a cute high school...romp, or whatever, but
it turns out to be about this girl who's a bimbo-but-we-
love-her. All she cares about is fashion, and make-up
but in the end, that's all she needs to triumph! And
I just started to weep. I had to leave. I was sobbing.
And outside, Frank is like "what?" So I have to *explain*
to him, that I feel fucking assaulted – that this is how
it *still* is in two thousand fucking seven in America.
Female power still comes down to knowing how to
apply under-eye concealer. And the biggest gesture of
self-love a woman can make is to get shot up with a
toxic virus that paralyzes her face, limiting her capacity
to non-verbally *express emotion.* Like this is something
women really want for themselves, like this is what
our mothers fought for – the right to live in fear that
our purse might not make a statement? I mean, how
much more productive would I be if I could wear the
same fucking shoes everyday and shaving my face was
my greatest act of personal hygiene? And now I have
to feel shame that I allow myself to appear in public
with a crease in my forehead? And Frank so brilliantly
rebuts that "the movie was a positive message about
having a career." Like we're supposed to stand up and
cheer that they're finally including a career in the
female fantasy of fulfillment? The point is, this chick
gets the guy. And it's because she has a tight ass, and
that's that. I don't care what little job they throw in
there. So then he does his "what's really going on
here?" thing. Which I resent, because it's like saying
my point isn't valid. But I have to tell him I'm getting sent to a "Bossy Broad Seminar." Have you heard
of this? It's disgusting. It's for women in power who

intimidate their co-workers, and don't get promoted, because their mealy-ass bosses are scared of having mommy keep her tit tucked into her fucking bra for ten hours a day. Excuse my language, but, my supervisor calls me into his cocksucking corner office and he says "Your staff is rebelling. You don't say hello in the hall." I'm like "Do you?" "Do you try to present things *nicely* all the time?" *(She is crying now.)* and Frank says he relates, because he gets all these memos about procedure and it all becomes about him. You know, like everything – *(She looks up.)* Oh, is it time? Well, that's it, in the end, everything is about him. But I'm just going to let go and hand it over to God and just *(sigh)*...let go. Thanks for letting me share.

End of Act One

ACT TWO

Scene Six

*(**RACHELLE** sits in the dark. She does her Novena, as if trying to put herself into a trance.)*

RACHELLE. HailMaryfullofgracetheLordiswiththeeblessed artthouamongstwomenandblessedisthefruit-ofthywombJesusHolyMaryMotherofGodprayfor ussinnersnowandatthehourofourdeathAmen.HailMary-fullofgracetheLordiswiththee...

*(**BERT** enters, holding a bouquet of flowers.)*

BERT. Shell?

RACHELLE.....blessedartthouamongstwomenandblessedis-thefruitofthywombJesusHolyMaryMotherofGodpray-forussinnersnowandatthehourofourdeathAmen.

*(**BERT** turns on the kitchen light. The florescence flickers. **RACHELLE** falls silent and blinks in the light. **BERT** hands her the flowers. She does not reach to take them. **BERT** puts them on the table. He gets a beer out of the refrigerator.)*

BERT. You want one?

*(**RACHELLE** shakes her head, no. **BERT** leans against the counter, not sitting.)*

RACHELLE. She was so young.

BERT. Not that young.

RACHELLE. Don't even.

BERT. I don't know Shelly.

RACHELLE. Out in the middle of the park.

BERT. I don't know why. It was the weather.

RACHELLE. Who else is seeing you? Out in public like that.

BERT. No one –

RACHELLE. Like a teenager in the grass. What is she, a waitress?

BERT. She's a student.

RACHELLE. Oh God.

BERT. But she went back. She's not a kid.

RACHELLE. A student.

BERT. She's thirty-two.

RACHELLE. Thirty-two and she can't find someone her own age? Some professor?

BERT. I'm sorry.

RACHELLE. What does she study?

BERT. Computers.

RACHELLE. Computers. You must have a lot to talk about.

BERT. I'm sorry.

RACHELLE. Thirty two. It's your daughter's age.

BERT. Theresa's twenty eight.

RACHELLE. It's the one time I'm glad she's estranged.

BERT. What are you talking about?

RACHELLE. What if she found out something like that?

BERT. How would she find out?

RACHELLE. I wish I wouldna known. I coulda never known.

BERT. Why were you even over there?

RACHELLE. I had a beauty appointment.

BERT. Over there?

RACHELLE. It was special.

BERT. You don't need to waste money on that stuff.

RACHELLE. God forbid I try to feel good about myself.

BERT. I'm saying you don't have to.

RACHELLE. You mean because what difference does it make to you? I might as well be your mother?

BERT. No, I'm saying you're beautiful already.

RACHELLE. Not enough for you.

BERT. Yes enough.

RACHELLE. Not enough for the part of you that's a man.

BERT. What part of me's not a man? My heart? My brain? My soul.

RACHELLE. Don't talk to me about your soul.

BERT. My soul never loved a woman but you. Or my heart. Or my brain.

(*RACHELLE sobs. BERT comes and kneels by her, putting his head in her lap. She strokes his hair, weeping. She clutches his hair.*)

BERT. Ow.

RACHELLE. I'm sorry.

(*He pulls away, she clutches onto him.*)

BERT. Quit it, Shelly.

(*She clutches.*)

RACHELLE. Why?

BERT. Let go of me, Shell.

(*He throws her off him.*)

RACHELLE. Why do you keep doing this to me? It just gets worse and worse.

BERT. Get up, now. Come on.

(*He gently pulls her up.*)

RACHELLE. I saw her bare legs. Now, I'll never be able to think of anything else.

BERT. She's nothing to me.

RACHELLE. I'd rather the strippers, the ones who aren't people. I'd rather pictures.

BERT. I'll stop with her. Alright? Shell? I'll stop with her.

RACHELLE. Please? No people? No more people.

(*BERT sits in a chair. RACHELLE puts the flowers in a vase.*)

(*LIGHTS FADE*)

Qualification #6

(**CORINNE** *sits in a chair.*)

CORINNE. Sometimes I just want to put him on a leash. I just want to put one of those big plastic collars around his head so he can't see anything but a funnel in front of him. I want to put one of those invisible fences around our house so when he crosses the line, an alarm goes off. I guess I wish he'd never gotten out of jail. He got caught exposing himself to women in the park. The fool had his favorite bench he went to time after time. Some female citizen got sick of seeing his no good little Richard hanging out there day after day, she put a video camera on him. Got him arrested. But for some reason she dropped the charges. All he got was a few nights in jail. I think she got to feeling guilty. Like it's her fault she's got this body out walking in shorts, running by with her boobs bouncing, poor guy. I had to get money from my dad for his bail. There's nothing my dad loves more than having something on me. Seeing me humiliated. It's hard to see where there's God in this. Except for Jesus. Wishing he didn't have to be the one to suffer for everyone's sins. All he ever did was try to help. All he ever did was good and he's the one who ends up there with nails in his feet. So far that's the only place I see God in any of this. I'm sorry. I just want the right person punished for once.

Scene Seven

(Dressed for evening but consciously casual, **ALLISON** *straightens her apartment. It's already very tidy. Feminine. The doorbell rings. She jumps a little. She opens the door.* **TRIP** *holds out a bouquet of tulips.)*

ALLISON. Oh.

TRIP. Hi.

*(***ALLISON** *takes the tulips and* **TRIP** *steps in. There is an awkward second which ends without a kiss.)*

ALLISON. Thank you.

TRIP. They're tulips.

ALLISON. I see.

TRIP. I remembered you said –

ALLISON. Right. I'll put them in water.

(She heads to the kitchen. He looks around.)

TRIP. It's nice, your place.

ALLISON. *(from off)* Small.

TRIP. A little, but you made it sound like two people couldn't even stand in here.

ALLISON. *(from off)* Well, it's not like your place.

*(***TRIP** *looks at Allison's CDs.)*

TRIP. We have, like all the same CDs, practically.

ALLISON. *(from off)* Yeah, I noticed that.

TRIP. That's so weird…. Dean Martin. My Mom loves him. Rickie Lee…"Pirates," man. I haven't heard this since college.

(He puts "Pirates" on. "We Belong Together" starts playing. **ALLISON** *comes back in with the tulips in a vase.)*

So, I went.

ALLISON. You did!

TRIP. Yeah.

ALLISON. Well, how was it?

TRIP. It was weird.

ALLISON. It was? Like how?

TRIP. Well, you know, it's just like those AA meetings you
see in movies, but it's smaller and people are talking
about some pretty sick shit.

ALLISON. Oh, so it wasn't…?

TRIP. I don't know. I mean, there were also a lot of guys
like me.

ALLISON. There were.

TRIP. Yeah. It was like, the whole spectrum. One guy got con-
victed for messing with kids and now he's not allowed
to leave his house. But then there were guys who were
totally normal. With good jobs – one guy's a partner at
the firm where I started. He's like me, in a few years.

ALLISON. What's their…problem?

TRIP. Same stuff, porn, you know. Prostitutes. Affairs. Inter-
net, porn, mostly. They have to shut down their email
accounts, which is hard, you know, if you work.

ALLISON. Yeah….

TRIP. And some of them can't watch TV or go to movies
anymore.

ALLISON. Because…?

(She starts rearranging the flowers.)

TRIP. It triggers them.

ALLISON. Network TV?

TRIP. Totally. The babes. The reality shows, like the one
with the playboy bunnies. One guy talked about that.

ALLISON. I'm not familiar. So what happens if they watch it?

TRIP. It makes then want to, you know…masturbate.

ALLISON. Right. And that's not okay.

TRIP. Not for these guys.

ALLISON. You know, I wondered, when I read about that…
isn't it better to do that, than to you know, hurt someone?

TRIP. Well, it can hurt. If you do it enough.

ALLISON. How much do people do it?

TRIP. A lot, some of them.

ALLISON. …like how many times a day?

TRIP. Many.

ALLISON. Don't they have jobs?

TRIP. They do it at their desks.

ALLISON. Cubicles?

TRIP. I don't know, Al. It's not allowed. It's like the first drink. It's the beer of sex addiction. You start with that, and then you need something else, something more.

ALLISON. It took me years to even be able to masturbate. (Uch, it's such an ugly word.)

TRIP. Why? You weren't raised Catholic.

ALLISON. It just never…interested me. I'd rather read. I only started doing it because all the magazines say you should. Women should. Get to know their clitoris, or whatever. Clitorises. Clitorae.

TRIP. Well if you're an addict, you're only allowed to have sex in a committed relationship. You can't do anything alone.

ALLISON. What if you're not in a relationship?

(**ALLISON** *tugs at a loose button on her sleeve.*)

TRIP. Then you lose. You get God. There's a lot of God. Which is weird for me.

ALLISON. Why? You know God.

TRIP. I don't talk to Him about this kind of thing.

ALLISON. You go to confession.

TRIP. Not since I was a kid. And that's not God, that's the priest. It's a whole other God these guys are talking about, I think. Like my God is part of the problem and their God is the answer. Like the good God is into spiritual sex, or something.

ALLISON. It sounds great. Are you going back?

TRIP. I don't know.

ALLISON. Why not?

TRIP. Because where do you draw the line? I mean, do you
know how many porn web-sites there are out there?
Like five billion. All guys do this stuff.

(**ALLISON** *gets a small sewing kit from a drawer.*)

ALLISON. So you're going to web-sites now?

TRIP. No, I'm just saying. It's Out There. It's unavoidable.
Even if you throw out your porn. You still get emails
from "I'm a Ho.com."

ALLISON. I don't.

(**ALLISON** *gets a small sewing kit from a drawer.*)

TRIP. And it's not like I want to do it with kids, or anything.

ALLISON. Well, I wouldn't know who you want to do it with,
would I?

(*Threading a needle,* **ALLISON** *tries not to get upset.*)

TRIP. Well, I don't.

ALLISON. Yet.

TRIP. What does that mean?

ALLISON. It gets worse. That's what I read. It gets worse if
you don't do something.

TRIP. If you have it. If you are one.

ALLISON. You got a fifteen on the test!

TRIP. You took the test for me.

ALLISON. We went over it together.

TRIP. And it was thirteen.

ALLISON. Ten is a serious problem! (*pause*) And you said
there were guys like you there. (*pause*) But if you don't
want to go back, don't go back. It's not my problem.
(*She works on sewing her button.*) Is that what you came
over to tell me?

TRIP. You look pretty.

ALLISON. Oh come on. Now I look pretty? When I'm giving
up on you?

TRIP. I came over because I wanted to tell you that I went.

ALLISON. Okay, well, that's great.

TRIP. Because I feel like I want to tell you everything. Like you're the person I want to come to.

ALLISON. Like what though? Like a friend? Your best friend?

TRIP. Like when I met you, I already knew you. Like I've known you my whole life. Like I want to go through things with you.

(*TRIP reaches for* **ALLISON** *and they kiss.*)

See?

ALLISON. Yeah, but then what?

TRIP. I don't know…maybe, it'll get better.

ALLISON. If you keep going to those meetings, it might.

TRIP. I'll go again.

ALLISON. Go to a few. Go a lot.

(*She looks at him searchingly.*)

TRIP. My father is cheating on my mom.

ALLISON. Oh. No.

TRIP. Yeah.

ALLISON. Does she know?

TRIP. He's been doing this my whole life.

ALLISON. With the same woman?

TRIP. No. They never last. That's why my mom hangs on, you know, because in the end, he always comes back to her.

ALLISON. It's sad, she doesn't think she deserves better.

TRIP. And her poodle stopped eating.

ALLISON. There's a little dog in the middle of all that?

TRIP. Yeah.

ALLISON. Well, I'm sure the dog is depressed. Poodles really internalize. My mom was the same way. Always desperate for my dad's attention. She would get all these pets, then abandon them, because she didn't really want to take care of anyone else.

TRIP. You don't have any pets.

ALLISON. No. The building. I told you.

TRIP. But not even a turtle or something?

ALLISON. It's okay. I work with animals all day.

TRIP. You know…there's a meeting for you, too.

ALLISON. For me?

TRIP. For wives. Or partners, I mean.

ALLISON. Well, I'll go, if you decide you are one.

TRIP. You think I am.

ALLISON. …Yeah?

TRIP. So, you should go.

ALLISON. Not if you think you're not.

TRIP. It's not about me.

ALLISON. Yes it is.

TRIP. That's not what they say. You being with someone you think has a problem means you have a problem.

ALLISON. Well, that's stupid.

TRIP. Your last two boyfriends drank too much you said. And one of them cheated on you, didn't he?

ALLISON. So what?

TRIP. So maybe there's…a pattern.

ALLISON. That it's hard to find a decent boyfriend in this town.

TRIP. Maybe you choose men that will hurt you.

ALLISON. Are you saying you're going to hurt me?

TRIP. I don't want to. I love you.

ALLISON. You do? Do you?

TRIP. Yeah. Do you feel like…you could love me?

ALLISON. I don't know. Yeah…I mean, I did.

TRIP. Because, you know, nothing's perfect. Like, this idea that you can find someone and everything is perfect? But really, for most people, it's one or the other.

ALLISON. One or the other, what?

TRIP. That you really like someone, love them, even, or you're really hot for them. It's one or the other.

ALLISON. I don't know…

TRIP. Have you had both?

ALLISON. For a while, it's both. At first…it's always both.

TRIP. But then later, you realize that one thing was out-weighing the other so you convinced yourself it was both, but really it was Love or Hot For?

ALLISON. Maybe. Yeah. Maybe it has always been one or the other.

TRIP. And it's like, which is more important, you know? I've had the sex thing and it just, you know, it doesn't last, or it doesn't matter after a while. And everyone says, marry your best friend. Through kids and old age and whatever, it's not about sex. Maybe sex isn't even that important.

ALLISON. Maybe…

TRIP. And the other thing is so strong here, isn't it? The Like thing? The Love thing? I just, from the moment you walked in and started reaming me out about the cat, I felt like, this is it. This is the kind of woman, the woman, maybe, I want to be with forever.

(**TRIP** *kisses* **ALLISON**. *It's an emotional passionate kiss.*)

ALLISON. Hey!

TRIP. Shh. Let's just enjoy it.

(*They continue making out, undressing each other as the LIGHTS FADE.*)

Qualification #7

(**TRISH** *sits in a chair.*)

TRISH. Like four years ago my therapist – I went into therapy because I was in this horrible relationship with this
guy who lied to me all the time, and my self-esteem
was just in the toilet, surprise, surprise. So I finally
managed to leave this asshole but I was totally miserable and desperate and convinced I was too old to ever
find love and that I'd never have a baby. It was just
crippling Spinster Anxiety. Anyway, she said when you
meet someone and they instantly feel familiar to you,
like you've known them your whole life, it's because
you have known them your whole life, you've been
dating different versions of the same person. And
they feel familiar because they are – like your family,
familiar. She said I had to start manifesting a better
sort of man in my life, like I didn't believe there were
any. I was like, face facts honey, there's not a million
great single guys wandering around out there just
dying to impregnate me. And she said, "you don't
need a million. You just need one." But you have to
know what you're looking for to be able to find it. So
she told me to make a list of everything I wanted in a
partner, a "My Partner is..." list, and she said, "don't
edit yourself, because you think it's impossible to have
everything you want" – because of course, I thought
you can't have "sexy" and..."nice" on the same list
because they cancel each other out – some qualities
just don't show up in the same man, like "successful"
and "considerate." I was scared to put down "funny"
for example, even though I really like a funny guy,
because it always went hand in hand with "highly neu-
rotic," in my experience. Anyway, she said I could have
an A list for qualities that were vital, like, you know,
"capable of telling the truth." And a B list for things
that were negotiable, like "enjoys my family." I mean,
come on, we're looking for a human. And she was
like "be specific because this is really powerful. Don't

write something like "handsome," write "attractive to *me*" because it's not like you want a guy who everyone in the world wants to sleep with – it's better if you're the only one who does, right?" So, I made my list and I thought it was really comprehensive and two weeks later, I met Jake. And he totally filled the A list and a lot of the B and I thought, this therapist is a fucking genius. Anyway, last week I looked at this stupid list and I saw "treats me well" right there at the top where it should be. And I realized I don't even know what it means: "treats me well". I'm so used to settling for what I can get, I think the fact that he paid for dinner on our first date means he treats me well, and meanwhile, he can look at other women when we're walking down the street, he can cancel plans at the last minute, he can tell me I wasn't dressed fancy enough for his mother's stupid seder, and I don't even, like, factor that in. And you know. Maybe it's my fault. Because those guys who would look at me with that look, like everything I said was so brilliant and amazing, those guys who would bring me baked goods at work – they always repulsed me. And they're the ones I'm supposed to be dating? I'm not sure I can. I mean, I'm sorry. I really don't want to. Alright, I'm done. I'm done. Who wants to go next?

Scene Eight

(In **RACHELLE**'s *kitchen, peony, a dirty white poodle, her coat like overgrown topiary, lies on the floor.* **ALLISON** *kneels down and offers peony her hand to smell.)*

ALLISON. Poor thing. Poor little thing.

RACHELLE. You think? It's bad?

ALLISON. How old is she?

RACHELLE. Old. But not *that* old.

ALLISON. She looks about…eight?

RACHELLE. Oh dear. We got her…my husband got her for me, when my son moved to the city. So, it was…

ALLISON. Ten years ago.

RACHELLE. Actually, there was another dog first. A terrier. Tommy. But he was very cold. That was the last thing I needed. We gave him to my cousin. Peony came a few years later.

ALLISON. When did you notice the depression?

RACHELLE. Depression? She lost her appetite, I said. I never said she's depressed.

ALLISON. Okay. I'm sorry. I assumed.

RACHELLE. I never said she had that kind of a problem.

ALLISON. I'm sorry. When did she lose her appetite?

RACHELLE. I don't know, it's been gradual. A gradual lack of interest.

ALLISON. Has there been any other…unusual behavior?

RACHELLE. Well, look at her. *(pause)* She lost her will to live. She lost her personality.

ALLISON. What was she like…before?

RACHELLE. Very upbeat. Hopeful. Not like your average poodle, at all. She was spunky and…loving. Now, I can't even get her to the hairdresser. She won't stand it. Look how raggedy all her little poofs are.

ALLISON. Maybe she's just ready for a new look. A more natural look.

RACHELLE. It's a mess.

ALLISON. I like a natural poodle. It's more dignified for a mature gal like Peony.

(RACHELLE *tears up.*)

RACHELLE. Thank you. That's a nice way to look at it.

ALLISON. But we do want her to eat. Do you ever give her food you've made yourself?

RACHELLE. Dog food? I don't eat dog food.

ALLISON. Of course not. There are just a lot of studies that suggest that the food we make for ourselves – the left-overs and the scraps are far more nutritious than the commercial dog foods – because they're so processed.

RACHELLE. Well then.

ALLISON. I have some literature I'll leave with you. (*She takes out a note pad and writes.*) And I'm putting her on an herbal anti-depressant.

RACHELLE. Oh dear. I don't know about that.

ALLISON. I think it will help.

(RACHELLE *sighs.*)

Has there been…stress in the house?

RACHELLE. Like what? For Peony? No. I'm very good to her!

ALLISON. I'm sure you are. Obviously. You called me.

RACHELLE. My son told me to. He's paying.

ALLISON. Still. I meant…has there been stress…for you?

RACHELLE. No. Why? What do you mean?

ALLISON. Animals pick up on the environment. For ex-ample, I had a cat, many years ago, and when my boyfriend and I fought – we had a terrible fight, I had to move out, and my cat, well, she'd really been our cat, we raised her together from a kitten. Anyway, kitty jumped out the window. She killed herself. She com-mitted suicide. Because of the stress and the pain. In the house.

RACHELLE. That's horrible.

ALLISON. It's why I went into Animal Psychology, actually. I didn't want anything like that to ever happen again. Not just to me, but you know, to anyone.

RACHELLE. I have window guards.

ALLISON. Right. And that's good.

RACHELLE. Why didn't you have window guards?

ALLISON. We didn't know. And, honestly, the kind of windows we had…they were very big, those flat – we didn't know.

RACHELLE. Cats fall out the window every day. It's not suicide. It's the wind.

ALLISON. This cat was very agile.

RACHELLE. It's the wind.

ALLISON. I don't think so. In this case. It was the stress. In the relationship.

RACHELLE. What did my son tell you?

ALLISON. Well, he did…it's not that he said – I just got the feeling that maybe, it's been a difficult time for you.

RACHELLE. I don't even know you. He just met you a few weeks ago.

ALLISON. Several months, actually.

RACHELLE. We're a very private family.

ALLISON. Of course. Really, he didn't say…it's more, I just, I feel like I understand. It's something I can sense.

RACHELLE. What do you sense?

ALLISON. Pain, I guess.

RACHELLE. Pain?

ALLISON. I'm sorry. I shouldn't have said anything.

RACHELLE. What are you talking about, pain?

ALLISON. I just meant, the way, maybe that you get treated.

RACHELLE. I get treated fine.

ALLISON. You're a beautiful woman.

(**RACHELLE** *starts crying.*)

RACHELLE. Please, don't.

ALLISON. I'm sorry. I see a woman who deserves to be cared for, to be adored and treated like a queen.

RACHELLE. Oh honey. Oh sweetie.

ALLISON. You do. You do deserve that.

RACHELLE. You're so young. You're so so young. Men don't change. They don't have to. So they don't.

ALLISON. They do have to if we make them.

RACHELLE. How? One of us walks out, another walks in. It's the tragedy of biology. I walk out, the girl with the smell walks in and then in twenty years she's me. She's me twenty years ago. This girl could have been my daughter. Soon she'll be me.

(**ALLISON** *stares into space.*)

(*LIGHTS FADE*)

Qualification #8

(The women who have spoken sit in a circle. As **MARY**
speaks, **ALLISON** *pulls up a chair.)*

MARY. Hi, I'm Mary. I'm an Alcoholic-Over-eater-Debtor-
Incest Survivor-Co-dependent-Co-sex-addict, recovering
in this program. I know a lot of you already know my
story, but today is my three year anniversary and I'd
like to tell it again, just so I can remember how far I've
come. And every time I say it, it becomes more sort of…
common to me. More like a thing that just happened…
things that just happen. *(She sighs.)* Okay. Both my parents drank, but it was just in that way that it seemed
like everyone in our world drank, you know a cocktail
hour sort of thing that they always say is "generational."
Anyway, after my parents got divorced – it was like an
iceberg splitting from some warm current in the water
working it's way up over centuries…When I stayed with
my dad, he always put me in his bed. No one ever ques-
tioned this. My brother slept on the couch in this weird
little SRO my Dad got in the suburb we lived in, it was
near the train station and I remember he never had any
forks, for some reason. We would eat eggs with a spoon.
So the logic was that my brother was older, I don't know.
I slept with Daddy and you know, it wasn't always such
a restful sleep. I used to think of it as The Nightmares.
I guess that's what he would say in the morning, that I
had a silly dream that Mommy wouldn't understand,
or something. And you know, I missed him. I did. So,
I figured this was what happened when your parents
split up and your daddy moved into a bad carpet apartment with soiled linoleum and moldy tile. I guess this
was where I got the idea that I was a comforter, you
know, like a blanket that got wrapped between a man's
legs so he can feel some kind of softness, some kind of
warmth at night. I don't know. But I started drinking
and binging on food and drugs and whatever I could
get my hands on and, you know, that's what we all did
in high school, so who notices? And I tended to pick

the men who would use me that way, you know.... But I got sober from booze and drugs, and then I tackled the food issue – you know with an addict, you put down one thing and then pick up another. One addiction to the next, it's like a path that leads you back to the original...sin, I guess you could say. Because after all this work, you know five or more meetings a week sometimes, I finally met this amazing man who'd been sober ten years in AA, and I was in Al-Anon, and I thought, you know, I was done. Finally. You know? But no. I went to donate blood and they told me I was HIV positive. I thought, I must have gotten it some other way, from touching some infected person with an open wound. Yeah, well. I guess I did. So this led to, you know, the most brutal moment of my life. When I had to hear the confession from him. My whole life just crumpled like some logs after the fire's gone through them and it's just dirt. Anyway, it didn't take long to find this program and get to the actual bottom of things. It's like falling through this tower of cardboard floors. You hit bottom five times, and every time you drop a level the floor gets harder until you can really feel it. So, I have to be grateful and thank God for being the stone and the pillow. I can feel pain today, and I know it won't kill me. I could even die today and I know it won't kill me.

(silence)

OTHER WOMEN. Thanks, Mary.

ALLISON. Hi, I'm Allison and I feel sort of trivial after that. I'm not really sure why I'm here...*(pause)* My boyfriend said my being with someone who has a problem means I have a problem. I guess, he heard that in his meeting? Like, there's something wrong with me for wanting to be with someone like him? It's just...I'm thirty five. *(pause)* And people do change, don't they? I mean, if he really tries, he will, won't he?

(No other words come out of her mouth.)

OTHER WOMEN. Hi, Allison. Welcome.

(FADE OUT)

Scene Nine

*(Darkness, Rachelle's kitchen. **BERT** stands in the shadows, behind the yellow curtains around the window. He is transfixed by something across the way. His mouth is slightly opened. He parts the curtains stepping into the light of the window. He is naked. He holds himself. **RACHELLE** flips on the kitchen light.)*

RACHELLE. What are you doing?

BERT. Turn that off. TURN IT OFF!

*(Frightened, **RACHELLE** flips off the light, returning the room to darkness.)*

RACHELLE. What are you doing?

BERT. Nothing. Just standing here. I couldn't sleep.

*(**RACHELLE** steps toward the window. **BERT** blocks her.)*

RACHELLE. What?

BERT. Stop it, Shelly. I'm just standing here.

(She struggles to see around him. She sees what he sees out the window.)

RACHELLE. Is this what you do?

BERT. I can't help it if I couldn't sleep and that's going on over there.

RACHELLE. You get up for it, don't you. You wait until she comes home.

BERT. I don't know that person.

RACHELLE. You know her window. Don't you?

BERT. I just came in for some juice. I was thirsty.

RACHELLE. You're naked.

BERT. I was hot.

RACHELLE. You never sleep naked.

BERT. I was hot.

RACHELLE. You can't do this to people, Bert.

BERT. What was I doing? She's the one parading around – you think I'm the only man in this neighborhood who noticed?

RACHELLE. You can't do this. This is our home.

BERT. I'm sorry.

RACHELLE. I deserve better than this.

BERT. I know. I know.

RACHELLE. I can't be treated this way. I won't be treated this way.

BERT. I'm so sorry.

RACHELLE. This is where I draw the line.

BERT. I don't know what else to do.

RACHELLE. Keep it away from me. You keep it away from my home.

(He cowers in the corner. She puts an apron over him. He starts crying.)

Qualification #9

(**JANICE** *sits in a chair.*)

JANICE. *(She exhales.)* I'm trying to align myself with my
higher power right now. It's hard. *(She exhales again.)*
I'm Janice. I've been in this program four years now.
Still married to my husband. And what's changed? A
lot. Our marriage is tender and intimate and safe, now.
I have a relationship with God now. I couldn't even
say "God" with a straight face before. I'm Jewish and
my parents were affected by the Holocaust in that way
– they could never believe in a higher consciousness
after that. What kind of God would not only create
Hitler but would let him...thrive, in the way that he
did? And for most of my life, I've been so sheltered,
it's disgusting really, how little suffering I've known. I
mean, we can all feel bad about the fucked up things
our families did to us that got us into this room, and
it was by no means an idyllic childhood, but ever since
this happened with my husband, I mean, after the ini-
tial pain of "why me?", I started really taking in what
was happening in the world – making an effort not to
tune it out. Genocide, ethnic cleansing, government
sanctioned rape. This...Evil that's always with us. And
people talk about terrorists or whoever, like "they're
Evil," "this is the face of Evil." But, you know, obviously,
that's how they see us. I mean we're out there killing
children, torturing people, making the world "safe"
for "freedom" whatever the hell that means. The truth
is that the terrorists, the torturers, the rapists – they're
us. Not "America." But Us. You and me. Us. They're
us in very stressful circumstances. Bin Laden. Hitler.
Dick Cheney. They're us, in so much pain, the humanity just clicks off. Sorry, I don't mean to get political, I
know I'm breaking the rules – should I stop? *(Silence.
She looks over at the timer.)* All I wanted to say, and I feel
this is relevant, is that when we pass a beggar in the
street, when we can't face that we are financing the
slaughter of innocent people right now, our humanity

is clicking off. When someone looks at a naked child and gets excited, his humanity is clicking off. When any one uses the body of a prostitute, his humanity has clicked off. We can't forgive in others what we can't see in ourselves. I know I have to wrap this up. But what I've realized is that it's not a question of how God could allow children to see their mothers get raped. Because that's not where the God is. The God is in the love those mothers have for those children, the God is in the possibility that those children might one day be able to forgive. And in their forgiveness, hate is replaced by love. Hate is replaced by love. I don't think God is everywhere, everything. I think God is where Love is. So much of the time we have to bring God somewhere it's been wiped out. Sorry, did I go over?

Scene Ten

*(**ALLISON** and **TRIP** are in bed. He rolls away.)*

TRIP. Sorry. I'm sorry.

ALLISON. What do you mean? It's fine. It was good…

TRIP. I don't know. I got scared.

ALLISON. Of what? I mean, what were you thinking?

TRIP. Just…it was just this, I can't describe it…fear.

ALLISON. Just fear?

TRIP. And nausea.

ALLISON. But it's been going so well…hasn't it been better?

TRIP. Yeah, I guess.

ALLISON. Trip it has. We've been, it's been…passionate.

TRIP. It's so hard for me to tell. It's so different from how I'm used to it feeling…

ALLISON. Right. It's a transition. You have to redefine sex for yourself. It's not supposed to feel like a drug.

TRIP. Yeah.

*(**ALLISON** reaches for **TRIP**. They make out and for a moment things seem okay. Then **TRIP** pulls away.)*

Fear.

*(Long silence. **ALLISON** sighs, tortured)*

Do you want to talk about how you're feeling?

ALLISON. Why?

TRIP. Maybe it would help.

ALLISON. I feel…like I want to die. Like I wish you would just stab me in the gut, or put a pillow over my face and smother me once and for all.

(pause)

TRIP. You know they say it takes years. Three years or more. To get better. And then for the rest of your life you have to deal with it. There's guys in there who have been in recovery for twenty years, and one of them just had a slip.

ALLISON. There was a woman who thanks God that her husband is a sex addict because realizing it brought them both to all these deep understandings about themselves and now they have this incredible intimacy and meaningful healing sex…

TRIP. What's her name?

ALLISON. Cheryl, I think.

TRIP. Married to Keith?

ALLISON. I think, yeah. What? He doesn't think they have incredible intimacy and meaningful healing sex?

TRIP. He just doesn't put it that way. I get the feeling it's hard for him. She has some pretty intense issues herself.

(pause)

ALLISON. Nothing like that ever happened to me.

TRIP. Like what?

ALLISON. Like a lot of them have some…thing, some bad sexual thing that happened. Or they were raised with weird religious things. They all have some reason they end up with men like this. I don't think I have anything like that.

TRIP. Are you sure?

ALLISON. Even, one woman talked about covert incest? I think it's like, the parent treats the child like his lover, but never…does anything. Just like, "you're the only one who understands me" or whatever.

TRIP. Like my Mom. "You're my handsome guy." "You're my man."

ALLISON. Yes. But my father never did anything like that. He avoided me, really. He was too busy having sex with his assistants.

TRIP. Well, that's something…

ALLISON. It was the seventies! Everyone was having sex with their assistants.

TRIP. Yeah and now everyone jerks off in front of their computers, it doesn't make it good.

ALLISON. I read this study in the Times that said if you ask people if they were sexually abused as children, most will say "no." But if you ask the same people if they ever experienced "unwelcome sexual activity?" a lot of them say yes. One in three women! It's like no one sees that unwelcome sexual activity is abuse!

TRIP. So, you're saying you...?

ALLISON. I was thinking of you.

TRIP. Maybe you should start thinking of you.

(The door bell rings.)

ALLISON. Is that the door?

(The door bell rings again.)

TRIP. What time is it?

ALLISON. Late. Two?

TRIP. I'm not answering it.

(A long ring. ALLISON gets up)

ALLISON. I'm going to see who it is.

TRIP. Don't open the door.

ALLISON. I'm just looking through the peep hole. God!

(She goes to the door, looks through the peep hole. Then runs back, scared.)

It's your mother.

TRIP. My mother?

ALLISON. Yes!

TRIP. Well, let her in!

ALLISON. You let her in! I'm not even dressed!

TRIP. What does she want?

ALLISON. I don't know.

*(**TRIP** gets up and goes to open the door.)*

TRIP. Mom?

RACHELLE. Did I wake you?

TRIP. Yeah…

RACHELLE. I'm sorry. Can I come in?

TRIP. What's the matter?

> (**RACHELLE** *comes in carrying a suitcase. She walks straight to the kitchen.*)

RACHELLE. Oh God.

TRIP. What's going on?

RACHELLE. Can I make some tea?

TRIP. Yeah, sure. I don't know what there is…

> (**RACHELLE** *puts a kettle on the stove.*)

RACHELLE. Your father's in jail.

TRIP. Oh my god. What happened?

RACHELLE. I don't know the details. I don't have the money for bail.

TRIP. What is it? How much is it?

RACHELLE. Twenty thousand dollars.

> (**RACHELLE** *looks through the cabinets.*)

TRIP. What did he do!?

RACHELLE. It's only that high because the girl has family in law enforcement. But I'm sure it wasn't that bad.

TRIP. He can call me himself, if he wants my help. You tell him to call me.

RACHELLE. *(holding a tea box)* What is this? "Women's Moon Cycle?"

TRIP. It's Allison's.

RACHELLE. What is it?

TRIP. I don't know. Something feminine.

RACHELLE. Is she here?

TRIP. Yeah, she's here.

> *(The kettle boils.* **RACHELLE** *waves her tea bag.)*

RACHELLE. Go ask her what this is.

> (**TRIP** *takes the tea bag and goes to the bedroom, where* **ALLISON** *is standing at the door, listening.* **ALLISON** *jumps as* **TRIP** *walks in, holding the tea bag.)*

TRIP. My mother wants to know what this is for. Women's Moon Cycle?

ALLISON. It's for when you have your period.

TRIP. Is it safe to use if you're, you know going through the change?

ALLISON. I don't know. What's going on?

TRIP. My father got arrested.

ALLISON. Oh my god. For what?

TRIP. She won't tell me. So, no, you're saying, she shouldn't use the tea?

ALLISON. Don't we have anything else?

TRIP. I have no idea. You're the one who brings tea into the house.

ALLISON. Well, let me find her something else.

TRIP. Okay, but don't –

ALLISON. What?

TRIP. I don't know. Just don't, talk to her too much. She's very fragile.

(ALLISON *leads the way back into the kitchen, where* RACHELLE *has removed most of the dry goods from the cabinets.*)

ALLISON. Hi.

RACHELLE. Hello, dear. I hope I didn't get you up.

ALLISON. Oh no, of course not. It's good to see you. *(pause)* I don't think this is the best tea for you.

(She opens a drawer.)

We have chamomile, which might be nice for you. Tension Tamer? Earl Grey? Mint?

RACHELLE. Do you have something fruity? A fruity tea?

ALLISON. Oh…nothing fruity. No.

RACHELLE. Lemony? Or a rose hip?

ALLISON. No, sorry. Just chamomile, which is very relaxing.

RACHELLE. I'll have the Earl Grey.

ALLISON. Okay.

TRIP. Can you at least tell me what the arrest was connected to?

RACHELLE. My life as I know it is over.

TRIP. What happened to your savings?

   (**RACHELLE** *shakes her head.*)

RACHELLE. He spent it.

TRIP. On what?

RACHELLE. I don't know. Bad investments?

TRIP. He doesn't believe in investing.

   (**RACHELLE** *shakes her head.*)

RACHELLE. I'm through. I just want to be near the one good thing that happened in my life.

TRIP. Okay. Okay. Are you tired? Do you want to try to get some sleep?

RACHELLE. That's impossible.

TRIP. Well, Mom. I have to go back to sleep. I have work tomorrow.

RACHELLE. Fine. I'll just sit.

ALLISON. I can stay up with you. If you'd like some company.

TRIP. You have work, too.

ALLISON. Not until later.

RACHELLE. Oh, you don't have to dear.

ALLISON. I don't mind at all.

   (**TRIP** *gives her a look. She ignores him.*)

TRIP. I really think we should all try to get some sleep.

ALLISON. It's fine. Your mom just needs to unwind a little.

RACHELLE. I do. I need to unwind.

TRIP. Alright, Mom. We'll figure it all out in the morning.

   (*He kisses* **RACHELLE** *and goes into the bedroom. A pause as* **ALLISON** *looks searchingly at* **RACHELLE** *and* **RACHELLE** *avoids eye contact with* **ALLISON**.*)

RACHELLE. I was thinking I might make pancakes.

ALLISON. Now? We don't have ingredients…

RACHELLE. I have some. I brought some with me.

ALLISON. For pancakes?

RACHELLE. I was going to make them for Bert. For breakfast. I couldn't leave it all…

(She unzips her suitcase and takes out some flour, baking soda, vanilla.)

ALLISON. …Bert?

RACHELLE. Trip's father.

ALLISON. I thought his name was Anthony. The Second.

RACHELLE. His middle name is Robert. None of them want to be called Anthony. Anthony the first was a monster. I wanted Trip's name to be James…He has milk, I'm sure. Eggs?

ALLISON. Yeah. I just bought some.

*(***RACHELLE*** removes a whisk from her bag, then a knife and some olive oil.)*

RACHELLE. I know. I just couldn't leave it all.

(She starts making batter.)

ALLISON. Is someone taking care of Peony?

RACHELLE. I'll get her tomorrow. She's fine for a few hours.

ALLISON. Do you want me to get her?

RACHELLE. I can't, with the cat. Tomorrow, I'll…figure it out.

*(***RACHELLE*** mixes batter.)*

RACHELLE. I don't know why God hasn't made him better. I have prayed. I don't know what else I can do.

ALLISON. You could pray for God to make you better.

RACHELLE. Me? I couldn't be more good. I couldn't be more what God wants.

ALLISON. God doesn't want you to be unhappy.

RACHELLE. He must. If I am.

ALLISON. Don't you think God wants everyone to be happy?

RACHELLE. If God wanted everyone to be happy, we'd all

be happy. He makes the decisions and we live with it.
Some people he gives a big house in Tampa and some
people he puts in the ghetto with rats in their crib.
God chooses for some to suffer. We just have to pray
one day we get some mercy.

ALLISON. I don't think God wants suffering. I think people
decide God wants it that way, so they don't have to do
anything about it.

RACHELLE. I thought you were a Catholic.

ALLISON. I'm not…really.

RACHELLE. So you're just coming up with your own ideas?

ALLISON. Shouldn't I?

RACHELLE. Not if you want things to add up. *(pause)* I
have nothing left. Just one son. One son in the whole
world.

ALLISON. What about your other children?

RACHELLE. My youngest is, uch, Trip's brother John. He
drinks, you know. He can't hold a job. He only calls
for money.

ALLISON. What about Theresa?

RACHELLE. We're estranged.

ALLISON. Why is that?

RACHELLE. I don't even know. She won't talk to us anymore.
The last time I saw her was her birthday five years ago.

ALLISON. She just stopped talking to you?

RACHELLE. She fell under certain influences. A young man
who turned her…who knows. There was some kind of
therapy and then nothing but accusations and anger.
She was never angry as a child.

ALLISON. Accusations?

RACHELLE. False.

ALLISON. About your husband?

RACHELLE. What business is it of yours?

ALLISON. It's my business because I have to deal with this
too, the repercussions, on your son.

RACHELLE. What repercussions? Of what?

ALLISON. Of the sickness. And the denial.

RACHELLE. What are you talking about?

ALLISON. These things run in families! If you don't face it, it just keeps going, it never stops!

(long painful pause)

RACHELLE. I'm going to wait for Trip to wake up. To make these.

ALLISON. Okay. *(pause)* Do you think you might be able to sleep? I'll get you a blanket.

RACHELLE. No. I'll just…is there a magazine I could look at? Does he get "Us?"

ALLISON. I don't think so. *(pause)* There are some books… there are some books you might want to read, actually. I'll get you a book.

*(**ALLISON** gathers a few books from around the apartment. One is about sex addiction. She hands them to **RACHELLE**, and goes back into the bedroom, gets back in bed and curls up around **TRIP**.)*

Qualification #10

(**RITA** *sits in a chair.*)

RITA. I don't want to just blame men for this. I know my partner feels his mother is as much to blame for his situation as he is. My friends from Cuba and my friends from France say the problem lies in sexual repression and the cultural institutions that depend upon it: Religion, Puritanism, Marriage,…. But haven't men been hungry for young women, and availed themselves of the young females of their own family since the beginning of time? And I refuse to accept that this is biology – this need to conquer, to dominate sexually. I find that to be a very…convenient model. Evolutionary biology without…evolution. Even if biology got us here, evolution should still be happening. The species must continue to move forward. I'm saying, there has *never been a time* when people honored each other in the way we're after here in this room. A time when heterosexuality was a mutual expression between equally empowered partners. Equality has not even happened. Yet. Despite all the progress. And so we don't tend to realize that we are still settling for a definition of sexual freedom that has been circumscribed by male desire. Most of us don't have the slightest idea what sexual power is, on our own terms. Because I do not accept that our terms would produce educated young women whose greatest aspiration is to be downloaded in their underwear and who get hurt by hooking up but say that's how they wanted it... The only way to change the world, is to be able to see it, as it really is. To feel how it really is, right now. How does it feel? That's what I'm asking. How does it feel right now?

Scene Eleven

(ALLISON stands in the threshold of TRIP's door.)

ALLISON. What?

TRIP. Um, just…Uh, I'm trying to figure out where we should be.

ALLISON. What's – why are you acting so weird?

TRIP. No, it's just, my Mom is going to be back soon.

ALLISON. Oh. She's still here?

TRIP. Yeah. She's going to stay here for a little while.

ALLISON. …okay. Where is she sleeping?

TRIP. I put her in the bedroom. I'm out here on the couch.

ALLISON. Oh. Well, do you want to stay with me? If she needs a place? Or she could stay at my place and I can stay here?

TRIP. No, I think she really needs to be with me right now.

ALLISON. Okay…

TRIP. What did you say to her?

ALLISON. What did she say I said?

TRIP. You told her I was sick?

ALLISON. That's not what I said.

TRIP. She says you were attacking her.

ALLISON. I was not attacking her. I was helping her –

TRIP. It's not your family.

ALLISON. I never said it was –

TRIP. It's too much, Al.

ALLISON. Trip, she –

TRIP. I need some time off.

ALLISON. "Time off?" "Time off" what?

TRIP. Just, I don't know…it's too much for me right now.

ALLISON. What is?

TRIP. This. You. I need a break.

ALLISON. Oh. *(pause)* How long a break?

TRIP. I don't know.

ALLISON. Like a week? Or like, a month?

TRIP. I don't know. That's what I'm saying. I need some time off the clock with you.

ALLISON. The clock?

TRIP. I'm not saying it's over –

ALLISON. Oh, yeah, that would be a great a way to spend the waning days of my fertility – waiting around for a fickle sex addict to take me back.

TRIP. Woah.

ALLISON. I mean, you make it into me or your mother? And you choose your mother? Who got you into all of this in the first place?

TRIP. It's not about you or my mother. It's just – I had notes in that book, you know.

ALLISON. Like…what?

TRIP. Like, whatever, things I related to. Things about mothers.

ALLISON. Oh. No.

TRIP. Yeah.

ALLISON. I'm sorry. I thought…

TRIP. I know you wanted to help –

ALLISON. – maybe it's better, for her to see things as they are –

TRIP. Maybe you should worry about seeing things for yourself and not for my mother. Not for me.

(ALLISON *falls silent. Leaving the door open,* TRIP *goes to the bedroom.* ALLISON *stands. Tears fill her eyes.* TRIP *returns with the cat in a carrier.*)

Here. I want you to have her.

ALLISON. You're giving me Pussy?

TRIP. I think she'll be happier with you.

ALLISON. You're just giving your cat away?

TRIP. My mother's dog. They fight.

ALLISON. So you just give away your little cat.

TRIP. Do you want her?

ALLISON. Well, I don't want her out on the street.

TRIP. I can give her to someone else. I thought you'd want her.

ALLISON. She's a very special creature.

TRIP. I know.

> (*Suddenly teary,* **ALLISON** *takes the carrier and exits.* **TRIP** *falls into an armchair with a huge sigh. A moment later, he is asleep.*)

Scene Twelve

(ALLISON sits in a circle with the women who have qualified.)

ALLISON. Hi. I'm Allison, recovering in this program. Or something. Last week, I broke up with my...qualifier? He broke up with me, actually. I couldn't even do it. Things were so much better...I mean, they were, until they weren't. He's been going to meetings and he really seemed to be changing, I mean, he *is* changing. But it's like, it wasn't fast enough for me, or something.... I did such a stupid thing. A really terrible thing. *(pause)* I've always been drawn to people who need help, in some way. People I needed to help, I mean. It's like an instinct, really. I walk into a bar, a bookstore, a subway car, and if there's one guy there who's in abject pain, that's who I want. And he'll come right over to me. No matter how hard I try to see the red flags, he turns out to be...broken in some in some way and I have to fix him. Why? *(She sighs.)* So, okay. I got a sponsor. And she told me that every time I think about my boyfriend, and how I wish he would be, or... had been, I have to remember it's not him I have to change. It's me. She said I have to "become the person I want to be with." Which I love, because it's such a catchy phrase. Isn't it? So. If want to be with someone who is...not broken. I have to become...not...broken.

MARY. I want to be with someone I can trust. I have to become someone I can trust.

BECKY. I want someone who loves my body, the way that it is, I have to love it. The way that is is. *(She sighs.)*

CLAUDIA. I want someone who gives a fuck about other people. I have to become someone who gives a fuck about other people.

PAMELA. I want someone strong. I have to be...strong.

GRETCHEN. ...responsible.

CORINNE. ...smart.

TRISH. ...capable of intimacy with another human.

RITA. I want to be present.

GINA. There is someone living in the world right now, who is coming toward me like a message...

JANICE. ...of everything that I deserve now.

ALLISON. I don't have to save you. I save myself. I save myself.

(FADE OUT)

End of Play

Act One

#	Item	Character	Note	Type
1	Closet w/ doors #1		Built by scenic department See notes for contents	Set
2	Closet w/ doors #2		Built by scenic department See notes for contents	Set
3	Closet w/ doors #3		Built by scenic department See notes for contents	Set
4	Closet w/ doors #4		Built by scenic department See notes for contents No longer needs to have headboard built in	Set
5	Sink		Built by scenic department Not practical Curtains should open/ close (by hand)	Set
6	Refrigerator		Not practical With light With freezer	Set
7	Stove		Not practical w/ oven door and racks	Set
8	Window		With *curtains 431*	Set
9	Kitchen cabinets		One above *fridge 6* One above *stove 7*	Set
10	Bed (Queen size)		Moved in scene shifts With headboard that has shelf for items	Furniture
11	Coffee table		Moved in scene shifts Used in Trip's Loft and Allison' Apartment	Furniture
12	Loveseat	Trip	Must have arms Used in Trip's loft Used in Allison's apartment w/ *throw 362* for dressing	Furniture
13	Cube	Trip		Furniture
14	Kitchen table (round)		Used Rachelle's Kitchen w/ *tablecloth 173* Used in Trip's Loft w/ no dressing Moved in scene shifts	Furniture
16	2 Kitchen chairs	Rachelle		Furniture
19	Small side table	Trip	Used for Trip's Loft and Qualifications	Furniture
20	West Elm chair		Used for qualifications Used for Trip, Allison and Rachelle	Furniture
21	Wooden chair	Allison		Furniture
101	2 Pillows		For *bed 10*	Dressing
102	Bedding (Queen size)		On *bed 10* No bed skirt/ dust ruffle Blue fitted sheet and blue duvet cover	Dressing
103	Work bag	Allison	Contains *plastic bags 104, pad 111, pen 113, catnip mouse 105* and *mini dust pan 106*	Hand/ costume

#	Item	Character	Note	Type
104	Plastic bag	Allison	In *work bag 103* *Cat poop 110* goes in	Hand
105	"catnip" mouse	Allison	In *work bag 103*	Hand
106	Mini dust pan and hand broom	Allison	In *work bag 103* To clean up spilled kitty litter	Hand
107	Litter box		Contains *cat poop 110* and *litter109*	Dressing
108	Litter scooper	Allison	Plastic, possibly dirty looking Used to scoop *poop 110*	Hand
109	Kitty litter		Soiled w/ clumps In *litter box 107*	Dressing
110	Pieces of cat poop	Allison	In *litter box 107* Scooped into *plastic bag 104*	Hand
111	Pad of paper	Allison	In *work bag 103* Top edge w/ glue binding (for easy tear off)	Hand/ paper
112	Page	Allison	Ripped off of *pad 111* In *work bag 103*	Paper/ cons
113	Pen #1	Allison	In *work bag 103*	Hand
114	Money clip	Trip	In pocket	Hand
115	Money	Trip	In *money clip 114* (4- $50, 2- $20, 1- $10)	Paper/ cons
117	Cordless phone	Trip	Should look expensive On *side table 19*	Hand
118	Red wine bottle	Trip	Recognizably nice but not cliché	Hand
119	Red wine	Trip	liquid TBD- Allison and Trip drink	Consumable
121	Lid	Trip	On *wine bottle 118* Removed onstage	Hand
122	2 red wine glasses	Trip	Nice, Stemless wine glasses/ bistro style	Hand
123	St. Anthony Medal	Allison	Necklace	Costume
125	Mini lint roller	Allison	Easy tear-off tape	Hand
127	Throw pillow	Trip		Dressing
128	2 large books	Trip		Dressing
150	Purse contents TBD	Rachelle	In purse 472 (including wallet, tissues)	Hand
151	Baguette	Bert	Cut into slices onstage	Consumable
152	Bag	Bert	For *baguette 151*	Hand
154	Knife	Bert	To slice *baguette 151*	Hand
155	Cutting board	Bert	To slice *baguette 151*	Hand
156	Food items	Bert	In *fridge 6* For making crostini Not tomatoes, Includes extra beers	Consumable
157	Jar of pimentos	Bert	"Moldy" In *fridge 6*	Hand
158	Carton of eggs	Bert	In *fridge 6*	Hand
159	Eggs	Bert	In *carton 158* Boiled onstage	Consumable
161	Pot	Bert	To boil *eggs 159* w/ lid	Hand

#	Item	Character	Note	Type
162	Baking tray #1	Bert	For *baguette 151*	Hand
163	Nail polish	Rachelle	To fix *pantyhose 153* Clear	Hand
166	Ice cubes (fake)	Rachelle	To soothe Bert's burnt hand	Hand
167	Tray	Rachelle	Contains *ice 166*	Hand
168	Hand towel	Rachelle	For *ice 166*	Hand
170	Tea pot #2	Rachelle	In kitchen	Hand
171	Kitchen cabinet contents		TBD	Dressing
173	Tablecloth #2		For *kitchen table 14*	Dressing
174	Hot pads	Rachelle		Dressing
175	Centerpiece	Rachelle		Dressing
192	Porn movies	Trip	Various types, About 200 movies Some taken off shelf	Dressing/ hand
193	Porn movie #1	Trip	VHS Played in *VCR 195* In *VCR 195* (is ejected and put back in)	Hand
194	Porn movie #2	Allison	DVD	Hand
195	VCR	Trip	Practical	Dressing
199	DVD player	Trip	Practical	Dressing
196	TV	Trip	Audience may see porn images- Practical Should look expensive	Dressing
197	TV remote	Trip	For *TV 196*	Hand
198	Several garbage bags	Allison	To throw away *porn 192*	Consumable
228	Rachelle's Pen	Rachelle		Hand
229	Credit card statements	Rachelle	Several months' worth	Paper
230	Checkbook	Rachelle		Hand
231	Pile of receipts	Rachelle	Various sizes, Many receipts	Hand/ paper
232	Diet Coke can	Trip	Practical/ opened on stage- Trip drinks	Consumable
233	Dish rag	Rachelle	Used to wipe face	Hand
234	Ritz-Carlton hotel receipt	Rachelle/ Trip	In *pile of receipts 231* 8.5 x 11 size, tri fold	Hand/ paper
235	2 Drinking glasses	Rachelle	Used for *diet coke 232*	Hand
238	Cheese/ antipasto	Rachelle		Consumable
239	Plate	Rachelle	For *cheese/ antipasto 238*	Hand
270	Allison purse	Allison		Hand
271	Sex therapy books	Allison	3 paperback books (including *Sex Quiz 272*) Including one by Dr. Patrick Carnes Possibly *Out of the Shadows*	Hand
272	Sex Quiz	Allison	In soft back book (not from library) With questions from p. 55-61 printed on pages	Hand/ paper
273	Pencil	Allison	For quiz	Hand
274	White wine bottle	Trip	Nice but not cliché In *fridge 6*	Hand
275	White wine	Trip	Liquid TBD- Allison and Trip drink	Consumable

#	Item	Character	Note	Type
276	Cork		In *wine bottle 274* Removed onstage	Hand
277	2 white wine glasses	Trip	Nice, Stemless wine glasses/ bistro style	Hand
278	Belt	Trip	Puts on onstage	Costume
279	Wallet #3	Trip	On headboard of *Bed 10*	Hand

Act Two

#	Item	Character	Note	Type
311	Rosary	Rachelle		Hand
312	Bouquet of flowers	Bert	Held together w/ rubberband	Hand
313	Beer	Bert	Bottle w/ twist off top Practical/ opened on stage- Bert drinks	Consumable
314	Vase #1	Rachelle	For *bouquet of flowers 312*	Dressing
315	Broom	Rachelle		Hand
316	Pledge can	Rachelle	To dust table	Hand
317	Dusting rag	Rachelle	Scrap fabric	Hand
348	Compact	Allison		Hand
349	Lip gloss	Allison	Practical	Hand
350	Text books	Allison	Glued into shelves of *Closet 3*	Dressing
352	Bouquet of tulips	Trip	In plastic wrap	Hand
353	Several CD's	Allison	In cases Number TBD	Dressing
354	Pirates CD	Trip	Played in *CD player* 355	Hand
355	CD player	Allison	Practical Used to play *CD 354*	Dressing
356	Vase #2	Allison	For *bouquet of tulips 352*	Hand
357	Sewing kit	Allison	In *small box 361* Used to repair Allison's button	Hand
358	Hand sewing needle	Allison	In *small box 361*	Hand
359	Thread	Allison	In *sewing kit 357*	Hand
361	Small box	Allison	Contains *sewing kit 357*x	Hand
362	Throw	Allison	To dress *loveseat 12* in Allison's Apt Urban Outfitter's feel Should cover whole loveseat	Dressing
363	2 throw pillows	Allison	To dress *loveseat 12* in Allison's Apt Urban Outfitter's feel Should cover whole loveseat	Dressing
364	Small plant	Allison		Dressing
365	Make-up bag	Allison		Hand
391	Poodle	Rachelle	Stuffed (only partially seen)- breathing dog In *dog bed 392*	Dressing
392	Dog bed	Rachelle	For *poodle 391* With canopy structure to mask poodle	Dressing

#	Item	Character	Note	Type
			Light colored	
394	Literature	Allison	In *work bag 103*	Paper
431	Curtain		On *sink window 5* Sheer inner layer should open (by hand) Opaque outer layer	Dressing
471	Large canvas duffle	Rachelle	Contains pancake items	Hand
473	Tea kettle	Rachelle	Used to boil tea water	Hand
474	"Women's Moon Cycle" tea box	Rachelle	In *Closet 2*	Hand
475	Tea bag #1	Rachelle	In *tea box 474*	Consumable
476	Tea cup/ mug #1	Rachelle	For tea	Hand
477	Dry food items	Rachelle	In *Closets 1 and 2* Pulled out but not used	Dressing
478	Chamomile tea box	Allison	In *Closet 2*	Dressing
479	"Tension Tamer" tea box	Allison	In *Closet 2*	Dressing
480	Earl Grey tea box	Allison	In *Closet 2*	Dressing
481	Mint tea box #5	Allison	In *Closet 2*	Dressing
482	Tea bag #2	Allison	From *tea box 480*	Consumable
483	Tupperware of flour	Rachelle	In *Large canvas duffle 471* Used to make pancake batter	Consumable
503	Flour	Rachelle	In *tupperware of flour 483* Used to make pancakes	Consumable
485	Bottle of vanilla	Rachelle	In *Large canvas duffle 471* Used to make pancake batter	Consumable
486	Bottle of olive oil	Rachelle	In *Large canvas duffle 471* Used to make pancake batter	Consumable
487	Whisk	Rachelle	In *Large canvas duffle 471* Used to make pancake batter	Hand
489	Carton of eggs #2	Rachelle	In *fridge 6* Used to make pancake batter	Hand
490	Eggs	Rachelle	In *carton 489* Used to make pancake batter	Consumable
491	Mixing bowl	Rachelle	In *Large canvas duffle 471* Used to make pancake batter	Hand
495	Tea cup/ mug #2	Allison	For tea	Hand
496	Trip Blanket	Allison	For Rachelle to sleep on *loveseat 12* In *Closet 3*	Dressing
497	Pillow	Allison	For Rachelle to sleep on *loveseat 12* In *Closet 3*	Dressing
498	Milk container	Rachelle	Used to make pancakes	Hand
499	Milk liquid	Rachelle	Used to make pancakes	Consumable
500	2 Water glasses	Allison	For Trip/ Rachelle to drink from	Hand
501	Aspirin bottle	Rachelle	In *purse 472* Contains pills 503	Hand
502	Pills	Rachelle	In *aspirin bottle 502*	Hand

#	Item	Character	Note	Type
			Tic tacs	
504	Hand lotion	Rachelle	In *purse 472* Used by Rachelle Travel size	Consumable
505	Nutmeg jar	Rachelle	In *suitcase 471* Used to make pancake batter Containing nutmeg	Consumable
506	Water pitcher	Trip		
511	Cat carrier	Trip		Hand

Pre-Show

Item	1	2	3	4	5	6	7	Note
SR Props Table								
Trip's Eggs								
Rachelle's tea cup								
w/ tea bag								
Rachelle's box								
w/ receipts								
w/ Ritz receipt								
w/ credit statements								
w/ checkbook								
w/ pen								
w/ wet rag								
Trip mugs (2)								
Trip cups (2)								
Allison vase								
Rosary box								
Water pitcher								
w/ lid								
w/ water								
Peony								
w/ blue dog bed								
w/ white dog bed								
w/ screw driver								
w/ 2 D batteries								
Trip tea pot								
Stack of pots								
White tea pot								
Dish bin								
Trip money clip								
w/ 4- $50; 2- $20; 1- $10								
Women's Dressing Room								
St. Anthony's medal								
Apron								
Closet 1								
Mid-left door								
w/ red wine bottle								
w/ lid on								
w/ liquid in								
w/ 4 wine glasses								
w/ beer opener								
w/ 2 empty bottles								
w/ 4 martini glasses								
w/ 4 shot glasses								
Closet 3- Trip Side								
Top Left Door								
w/ porn dressing								
Mid shelf- Possessions								
Low shelf- removable porn								
Re-filled								

Item	1	2	3	4	5	6	7	Note
Closet 3- Trip Side								
Top Right Door								
w/ porn dressing								
Low Shelf								
w/ VCR								
On								
Tape rewind/ eject								
w/ spare video								
w/ DVD player								
w/ porn dressing								

Item	1	2	3	4	5	6	7	Note
SL Props Table								
Allison Work Bag								
w/ Pad								
w/ Pen								
w/ lint roller (side)								
w/ orange mouse								
w/ plastic bags								
w/ mini dust broom								
w/ mini dust pan								
w/ literature (front)								
3 sex books								
w/ pencil								
w/ quiz								
Allison plant								
Allison make up case								
w/ compact								
w/ lip gloss								
Allison purse								
Bert flowers								
w/ rubberband								
Trip tulips								
w/ cellophane								
Baguette (in bag)								
Cat carrier								
w/ bunny								
Rachelle bag								
w/ blue bowl								
w/ wisk								
w/ spatula								
w/ nutmeg								
w/ vanilla								
w/ olive oil								
w/ pink socks								
w/ bag of toiletries								
w/ tupperware								
filled w/ flour								
Allison throw								
Allison yellow pillow								

Item	1	2	3	4	5	6	7	Note
Closet 2								
Door masking US								
Lower-left door								
w/ cat box								
Filled w/ litter								
w/ poop								
w/ scooper in								
w/ Bag of litter								
w/ Yellow bag								
w/ cat toys								
Door propped open								
Closet 4- DS Side								
Top Center Door								
w/ books dressing								
w/ empty space								
Bottom Center Door								
w/ linen dressing								
w/ blue pillow								
w/ blue throw								

Item	1	2	3	4	5	6	7	Note
Closet 3- Trip Side (cont)								
Top Center Door								
w/ TV- OFF								
w/ remote								
w/ porn dressing								
Closet 3- Allison Side								
Low Left Shelf								
w/ sewing kit (cigar)								
w/ purple snips								
w/ red scissors								
w/ thread								
w/ needle								
Latch up								
Mid Left Shelf								
w/ boom box								
Off								
w/ CD in								
w/ case next to								
w/ volume all up								
Freezer								
2 empty ice cube trays								
Ice bin								
w/ ice								
Empty pie tray								
Baking soda								
Fridge Cabinet								
Tea cups								
Wooden bowls								
Plate dressing								

Item	1	2	3	4	5	6	7	Note
Stove Cabinet								
Top shelf								
w/ baking dishes								
Mid Shelf								
w/ tuna								
w/ cereal								
w/ alcohol								
Bottom Shelf								
w/ boxes dressing								
w/ 2 green glasses								
w/ silver tin								
w/ flour bag								
w/ 4 tea boxes								
Moon tea face US								
Counter btwn stove and sink								
Rachelle Purse								
w/ wallet								
w/ tissues								
w/ lotion								
w/ aspirin								
Stove								
3 silver canisters								
Salt and pepper and hour glass								
Rachelle vase								
Large pot (DSR)								
w/ lid								
w/ water								
Black tea pot (DSL)								
Centerpiece								

Item	1	2	3	4	5	6	7	Note
Closet 4- DS Side								
Bottom Center Door								
w/ Trip belt								
w/ Trip wallet								
Fridge								
Top Shelf Door								
w/ nail polish								
w/ D batteries								
Mid Shelf Door								
w/ pimentos								
w/ seltzer								
Bottom Shelf Door								
w/ 4 juices								
Top Shelf Inside								
w/ cake								
w/ Bert's eggs								
w/ coffee								

Item	1	2	3	4	5	6	7	Note
Fridge								
Middle Shelf Inside								
w/ beer carton								
w/ 3 beers								
w/ bowl of grapes								
w/ 1 can coke								
w/ baking soda								
Bottom Shelf Inside								
w/ 2 juices								
w/ parsley								
w/ coke box								
Outside doors								
w/ photos/ magnets								
Floor SR of Fridge								
Broom								
White wine bottle								
w/ cork								
w/ liquid								
Tin can								
White watering can								
Sink								
Lotion								
Sponge								
Dish soap								
White towel								
Stripey towel								
Speaker								
Saran wrap								
Counter under window								
Plant								
Toaster								
Drawer								
Paper towels								
2 red oven mitts								
2 blue hot pads								
4 wash cloths								
Extra stripey towel								
Extra white towels								
Extra Sponges								
SR Wing								
2 aluminum door covers								
Aluminum stove cover								

Item	1	2	3	4	5	6	7	Note
Cabinet Below Sink								
Trash can								
w/ liner								
Pledge								
w/ rag								
Spray cleaner								
Saran wrap box								
Dog biscuits								
Plastic bags								
Window Wall								
Curtains pulled back								
Rosary on hook								
Wall dressing								
DSR								
Side table- green								
Open DS								
w/ phone								
West Elm chair- green								
DSL								
Coffee table- green								
w/ 2 books								
Loveseat- green								
w/ owl throw pillow								
West Elm cube								
VOM SL								
Black chair								
VOM SR								
Red pillow								
Vom light down								
Real Fridge								
Milk								
Eggs								
Antipasto plate								
Extra antipasto ingredients								
Creamer								

Item	1	2	3	4	5	6	7	Note
Cabinet Below Counter								
Top shelf								
w/ tablecloth								
w/ baking tray								
w/ knife								
w/ cutting board								
Bottom shelf								
w/ feather duster								
w/ garbage bags								
w/ one bag free								
w/ 2 thermoses								
w/ pot and pan								
Rug on floor								
USL								
Kitchen table								
Kitchen chair 1								
Kitchen chair 2								
Closet 1- gray								
Closet 2- gray								
Closet 3- green								
USL								
Bed								
w/ fitted sheet								
w/ duvet								
w/ 2 pillows								
Neatly dressed								
Closet 4- green								
Crew								
Sound check								
Video check								
Dimmer check								
Head set check								
Cue light check								
Sweep								
Mop								
Run lights								

Also by
Kate Robin...

What They Have

Please visit our website **samuelfrench.com** for complete
descriptions and licensing information

Printed in the United States
214274BV00003B/4/P

9 780573 663079